FYNGAL'S GOLD

Sol Klein and Paddy Fyngal became closer than brothers. They were brought together by their mutual enemy, Black Jack Stillman, and the gold in the sacred Black Hills of South Dakota. The miners of the Black Hills had long suffered the tyranny of Black Jack and his cut-throat gang. Now Paddy Fyngal was fighting back as their leader with Sol close behind them. The war had begun!

TEX LANNIGAN

Complete and Unabridged

LINFORD
Leicester

First published in Great Britain in 1996 by
Robert Hale Limited
London

First Linford Edition
published 1997
by arrangement with
Robert Hale Limited
London

British Library CIP Data

Larrigan, Tex
Fyngal's gold.—Large print ed.—
Linford western library
1. Western stories
2. Large type books
I. Title
823.9'14 [F]   LP

ISBN 0–7089–5089–2

Published by
F. A. Thorpe (Publishing) Ltd.
Anstey, Leicestershire

Set by Words & Graphics Ltd.
Anstey, Leicestershire
Printed and bound in Great Britain by
T. J. International Ltd., Padstow, Cornwall

This book is printed on acid-free paper

1

THE huddled figure lying in the shade of the overhanging rock groaned and muttered in his sleep. He moved restlessly, a dusty sweated heap of rags that stank. He smelled of cheap rotgut whiskey and the hot pungent smell of chillies. He turned on his side to find a more comfortable position on the rough ground and his hat, protecting him from sun and flies, fell from his face.

He cursed, half awake by his own movements and groped for the black crushed hat that he'd had so long it was a part of him.

Then suddenly he was alert, his wits responsive and he was reaching for the Peacemaker that lay conveniently by his side. He could hear gunfire and a thundering of hooves.

He bellied over, looking down the

ridge of rock that already covered him, for he was holed up high in the Black Hills, having left prospecting for gold because of a dispute with a miner twice his size.

Black Jack Stillman! Was he still on his tracks? Three days it had been since the showdown with Black Jack and one thing he, Sol Klein, was sure of; apart from Black Jack's meanness, was his persistence to persecute any man who tried to rob him.

Sol had tried just that. He'd pocketed two large lumps of gold straight out of the bed of the creek. Trouble was, they came from Black Jack's claim and the bastard had eyes in his arse. He could smell trouble. Sol had been a gambler for more years than he liked to admit, but still Black Jack had read the thieving in his eyes. The upshot was that Sol had suffered a beating up good and proper and he'd been run out of the mining camp minus those cursed nuggets and then Black Jack had set his hound on him.

It was just Lady Luck smiling on him that hadn't seen Sol's end in the jaws of the wolfhound's mouth. The heavy-set beast had been lunging at him in a gut-churning attack when the ground had opened and it had plummeted into an ancient mine-shaft below.

Sol had been so relieved he'd laughed with pure joy and shaken his fist at the big man who was coming lickety-split on a slow-moving horse more used to pulling a wagon.

Then he'd scrambled away high up into the hills where he'd flung himself down exhausted many hours ago.

Now was the bastard on his trail again?

He watched as far down below the lone man on horseback was riding as if his life depended on the speed of his nag; and far behind, the moving specks that kicked up a dust which became larger by the minute. He counted six men and they too were covering the ground as if racing each other. He screwed up his eyes to see better but he didn't recognize the oncoming man.

The shots came more frequently as the pursuers slowly closed the gap between them. Sol saw that the oncoming horse was lame but still making a gallant effort, but the outcome would be inevitable if he didn't take a hand.

It was only a moment before he decided. No ifs or buts. This was action. He'd never liked to see the underdog fall under the heel of the oppressor. He whistled three short blasts and he saw the man look up the escarpment. He moved out of the shade and waved just as the horse beneath the man stumbled for the last time and fell with heavy ribs to the ground.

The man didn't hesitate. He drew his rifle from the saddle boot and a heavy leather saddle-bag from the pommel and after swinging the double bags over his shoulder swiftly tackled the incline and followed a faint track made by wild goats.

Sol ducked into the shadow of the overhanging rock. He guessed he would be almost invisible to the oncoming men who would have the sun in their eyes.

He watched while the man made good time. He could hear his beloved belaboured breathing. The man was about all in but fear and the adrenalin were keeping him going.

Then, calculating his chances of a hit, he coolly took aim with the powerful Peacemaker and waited for a strike even though the slugs were coming thick and fast. Fortunately the men were riding too fast to take careful aim. But Sol's first shot took the foremost horse in the foreleg and it rolled over, jack-knifing its rider over its head. The rest of the men lost stride and fanned out but Sol saw another man pitched from his saddle and lie still as he took several shots in quick succession.

Then Sol was leaning over the rim of the escarpment and pulling the man clear, watching as the four remaining horsemen stopped to parley and then turned around and trotted away.

The stranger grinned at Sol. He was a much older man than Sol and his wild untamed hair was a coarse black and streaked with grey as was his beard.

"Put it there, buster. You saved my life." The big man stuck out his hand and grasped Sol's in a grip that made Sol want to squeal. "I'm Paddy Fyngal and sure if I'd been a black cat I should have lost one of me lives! I would an' all!"

So the feller was an Irishman, was he? Sol had never liked Irishmen. They made remarks about Jews.

"I'm Sol Klein. What you been up to, Paddy Fyngal?"

Fyngal shrugged.

"Just a little argument with the law at Harper's Creek. That blackhearted assayer was suspicious about my gold, God rot him! Called in the marshal, he did and I had to banjo 'em all. As if it is any of their business, damn me, where my gold comes from!"

"But why should he be suspicious? Hundreds of men are queuing up to deposit gold, nuggets or dust. Why you be so different?"

Paddy Fyngal suddenly looked sly.

"Ah, to be sure, I was different. My gold was minted. I'll not lie to ye, boyo, seeing as we're together and you got those spalpeens off my back." He patted the two bags by his side. "Ten thousand dollars in that lot and there's more where that came from."

Sol Klein stared.

"You're joking!"

"Niver a divil of a bit of it! I don't joke about gold or women, God bless 'em."

Sol Klein marvelled. He was beginning to like Irishmen, or to be truthful, this Irishman. There were some he could name that he would swing for, given the chance.

"Did you rob a train or what?"

Fyngal grinned.

"I was a scout and guide for a

military wagon train taking the payroll to Fort Laramie. I was guiding them through a little known pass which was a shortcut to the fort when we were ambushed by Crazy Horse's dog soldiers. They fought like demons and were on us before we knew they were there. Our captain was shot but not before he gave orders for the gold to be stashed and I was the man who helped the corporal to hide that gold. Hiding that gold saved my life for as we left the cave where it is to this day, the corporal, God bless his soul, was knifed by one of those cursed Indians. The bastard started on Tommy's scalp and it gave me a chance to creep up behind him and stick my knife in his back. He grunted and I dragged him to the cave and left him there and I laid low until the fighting was over. Those warriors left no one alive and all that next night they were dancing and yelling fit to bust and I shivered and imagined what it would happen to me if they caught me. I prayed hard, I can tell you. Told God in no uncertain terms that if I lived through this lot I'd mend my ways and go to confession if ever I could find a priest."

"And how long since all that happened?"

"Seven, maybe eight years ago."

"And have you confessed?"

"Not yet. Never found a real priest but I will someday, just as surely as my father was called Fyngal!"

Sol wasn't so sure about that but he wouldn't risk insulting Paddy's mother. The Irish could wax sentimental over mothers. He knew that was right by all the songs he'd heard sung about the old country.

"What are you going to do now, Paddy? There's a mighty lot of gold to tote around."

He looked at the bags speculatively. He could have done with a handful of what was packed inside.

"Don't even think about it," came the soft Irish voice which held a note of menace. "I sleep with one eye open and my hand on my gun!"

"Sorry. Just wondering what a pile of gold eagles would look like, that's all, never seeing more than six at one go."

"Well, I'm not going to indulge you, boyo. Gold turns a feller's brain, that it does. Somethin' about the colour, I reckon."

Sol shrugged.

"What about trying to catch those two horses down there? One of 'em is lamed but he's on his feet so mebbe he's only nicked. The feller riding him must have broke his neck."

"Yeh, and I hope he goes to Hell! He was the marshal's deputy and a slimy little dungball. He was the marshal's eyes and ears. There'll be lots in Harper's Creek who'll celebrate his passin', goddamn him! I'll have his horse, it's just right and fittin'."

They scrambled down the escarpment and apart from jerking their heads aloft and twitching their ears, the two horses watched them move slowly near and finally allowed them to take the reins.

The deputy's horse showed a bloody foreleg but it was only a nick and once the wound was plastered with mud to keep off the flies, it would soon be good as new.

"Where we heading buster?" Sol thought it expedient to allow Fyngal to take charge. Better to keep the Irishman happy and he was in no mind to lose track of the rich bastard.

"We'll head for the fort."

"How about looking through these saddle-bags? They might have been carrying coffee and grub."

The saddle-bags yielded more than coffee and grub. They held spare shells for the rifles of the dead men.

Paddy Fyngal grinned at Sol.

"We're in luck, boyo. There's enough shells here to stock an army. No need to bribe the quartermaster at the fort. We can go in and stock up with grub and hightail it back to Harper's Creek."

Sol looked at him as if he was loco.

11

"What the hell we go back there for? I've just bust my guts to get away from that place. Black Jack Stillman is a man who doesn't give a man another chance."

"So you had a run-in with him, eh? What did you do? Take his woman or his gold?"

"Look, mister, does it matter?"

"Yes, it matters. If you messed with his woman, he might just kill you, but try and take his gold, then that is another matter entirely. He'll torture you first before he kills you!"

Sol swallowed a hard lump in his throat.

"I didn't know his reputation or I wouldn't have offered to work for him. I'm a stranger in these parts being on my uppers, like, and I thought he wouldn't miss a couple of chunks of ore. He was mighty slick. I think the bastard's got the instincts of a mountain cat! He smells trouble!"

"Aye, he's a wily bird. That's why he's turned out more gold than anyone

12

else. He hires gunmen for help and lets the miners work their claims and when they find a payload he sets his boys on and drives the poor sod off if he's lucky. If not, he becomes just another mound on Boot Hill."

"You sound as if you know a lot about him."

"Aye, to be sure I do! The marshal, Jed Payne is his brother-in-law, and the assayer, Bill Tomlin, is his lackey. Bill Tomlin is the only representative of the Gold Corporation Syndicate in these parts and everyone in Harper's Creek knows his gold has to go through him. He tells Stillman when there's been a good strike but the poor buggers haven't the guts to get together and get rid of the whole boiling."

"Yeh, I can understand that what with the gunmen and all. Why don't we just ride away? You've got the dough and I don't want to get involved in other folk's feuds."

"Smart little fart, aren't you? No backbone. Well, what would you expect

from a Jew! Looks both ways at once."
Paddy spat on the ground in contempt.

Sol straightened up, his face flushing. He was short and slight and always looked half-hungered so that his nose appeared larger than it was, but he'd never rated himself as a coward and could hold his own in a fight. What he couldn't contend with was a bearhug from a big feller, but his speed always saved him from that, ever since the day when he was just a fresh-faced youngster and cocky enough to take on a wrestler twice his size, and a bust rib had made him very aware of the importance of fancy footwork.

It looked as if this potato-face needed a lesson in the same fast footwork.

"You can take that back or I'll show you what I'm made of!"

Paddy Fyngal looked surprised.

"So the little cockerel can crow! Why, I could eat you up and spit out the bones in five minutes, sure I could!"

Sol's temper erupted. With little

thought he unbuckled his belt and dropped it on to the ground. His fingers twitched as he crouched ready to take on the bigger man.

"Come on, you Irish bogtrotter, let's see just how good you are."

"Don't be a fool! You saved me from the marshal. Never let it be said that Paddy Fyngal would crack the ribs of the man he owes his life to!"

"Come on, or have you got the jitters? You're wondering about me, aren't you? You know I must be good or I wouldn't be standing here begging you to have a go! You're the one with the yeller streak!"

"Why, you ... " Paddy lunged forward and Sol was grinning and leaping to one side but not before he stuck out his foot and Paddy went crashing down, helped on by a nasty jab to the neck.

"There, you Irish mick, first blow to me. Now stop gasping and get up and let's see what you're made of!"

Paddy looked up at him, his neck

numbed by the jab. He scrabbled in the dust as he watched the small lithe figure moving like a jack-in-a-box. He blinked and shook his head and then was up on his feet in a fast movement that fooled Sol for a moment. Paddy tore into him and Sol took two blows to the arm and the side of his neck, but Paddy couldn't get hold of him.

Paddy suffered two quick jabs and never saw them coming. They hurt and they infuriated him. He lashed out and any one of the blows would have laid Sol out flat. They never connected.

Sol took his time and placed his punches with care. It was like teasing a baby.

Then Sol became over-confident and Paddy had him. A jarring slam at Sol's head which slowed him down and Paddy was gripping him tightly and to Sol's horror he was swung high above Paddy's head and the big man slowly whirled him around until the whole world was swinging. Sol closed his eyes in anticipation of the big crunch and his life flashed before his eyes. He was thirty-six years old and had done sod all with his life and now to have his head bashed like an egg by a stinking Irish mick was the last straw.

He heaved and struggled and he could hear the growl of laughter in the mick's throat.

"Damn you, you son of a bitch!" he yelled. "Do what you have to do but get on with it. I'm not here to amuse you!"

The noise of Paddy Fyngal's laughter grew and rattled Sol's ears, and then incredibly, he was being lowered gently to the ground.

He stared up at Paddy who was grinning widely.

"What about some coffee, you circumsised prick? Did you really think I'd stove your head in?"

Sol sat up and rubbed his arms.

"Yes, I did. All the Irish bastards I've known have been queer tempered."

Paddy Fyngal reached down and grasped Sol by the throat and lifted him to his feet as easily as if he'd been a baby.

"Not so much of the Irish bastard, Shylock. We're touchy about our mothers. Now do you want coffee or not?"

Sol nodded. His belly rumbled. He could do with something solid in his guts but coffee was better than nothing. He went silently to find firewood and soon they had the deputy marshal's coffeepot singing on a forked stick.

While the coffee brewed, both men doused themselves in the small stream nearby and both inspected each other's bodies and liked what they saw. For though Paddy was big and wide he was muscled. There was no fat and Sol, although slim to the point of gauntness, had that stringy strength that spoke of endurance.

Their eyes met and suddenly they were grinning at each other.

Paddy cleared his throat.

"I still owe you, mister."

"No you don't. You had me fair and

square. You could have killed me and you didn't. So we're quits."

"Will you shake hands?"

Sol hesitated.

"I still don't like micks."

"Well, I don't like Shylocks but I'll shake with you."

"Very well. If you can force yourself, so can I."

Paddy stuck out his great paw and Sol took it gingerly, but this time Paddy didn't turn on the pressure.

"What say you and me ride together, boyo?"

"You mean, pards?"

"Aye, sure an' all, I mean pards. You're a good fighter for a little 'un. How about it?"

"You're still wanting to go after that marshal of yours?"

"Why not, just for the hell of it?"

"Do you enjoy fighting?"

"As sure as my mother was Connor Fyngal's true wife in the sight of God!"

"Well, I can't argue with that. Maybe we can be pards after all, especially if you deal me in for a share of that there gold!"

"Aha! I thought the gold might get to you! You can share what's in my saddle-bags, but I'll not tell the Holy Mother herself where the rest is stashed, so help me God!"

Sol shrugged.

"That's good enough for me, mister. A share of what's in those bags will buy a lot of loyalty. I even feel more like tackling Black Jack Stillman just for the hell of it!"

"Now you're talking like a man of my own heart, boyo . . . Come on, let's drink that coffee and be on our way to Fort Laramie. The storeman there stocks everything a man could want. A bath and a shave and new clothes and those buzzards back in Harper's Creek won't know either of us!"

They grinned at each other. Black Jack Stillman and his bunch of kow-towing hangers-on were in for a big surprise.

2

THEY drew rein at the point where they could see the whole of Fort Laramie spread out like some obscene scar on the landscape. Even from a distance one could see the huddle of buildings surrounding the stout timber walls, the coming and going of the hangers-on who follow the military.

They could see the store and the saloon, the rows of horses standing flicking tails in the sun, and the lounging renegade Indians who acted as scouts and spies for the fort.

Sol's horse moved nervously as if he sensed Sol's own nervousness.

"Are you sure we're doing right, Mick?" He spoke thoughtlessly. He'd been careful on their travels not to tread on Paddy's corns. Now the mick had slipped out unintentionally.

"Don't call me Mick! I warned you, Shylock!"

"Then don't call me Shylock. Understood?"

The two men glared at each other and then Paddy nodded.

"Done. I'll not call you Shylock to your face. How's that?"

Sol grinned.

"Then I'll only call you Mick behind your back. Right?"

"Right."

"Then now that's settled, you might answer me. Are we doing right, going in there? It's like putting your head into the lion's mouth."

Paddy laughed. "We'll be in and out before you can say Paddy M'Ginty's goat. A drink, a bath, new clothes and a belly-filler and a visit to the store and we'll be away before the military wake up."

"You're mighty sure of yourself, Paddy, but it's been four days."

"And what of it? The marshal and Stillman won't want all the territory

22

knowing about that gold! They'll want it for themselves. Oh no, it will be safe enough, or my name's not Paddy Fyngal!"

Sol smiled grimly.

"I hope your name is Paddy Fyngal. By the way . . . what's all this about Paddy M'Ginty's goat and who was this M'Ginty feller?"

"Paddy M'Ginty? Well now, he was a boyo back in Ireland, sure he was but it's a story as can wait until one dark night when I've got the time to tell it properly wit' a bottle in my hand for sure; the bottle makes me tell the stories better, that it does! Come on now, boyo, let's ride and put my theory to the test."

"What theory?"

Paddy threw Sol a pained look.

"Haven't I been after tellin' you? About the marshal wantin' to keep the gold a secret, an' all, an' all?"

"Oh!" Sol reluctantly followed Paddy's horse. He wasn't quite so convinced as Paddy was, even now, but as Paddy was a pard he had to follow where Paddy led.

They joined the throng of people going about their business at the fort. There were a couple of wagons being unloaded at the store and a column of soldiers just leaving on a tour of duty. A few Indian women stood around with bundles and a bunch of cowboys newly in from a long trail were hitching horses at the rail before stampeding the saloon.

There was noise of clanking metal coming from an improvised black-smith's shop, and farther along a row of tents which Sol guessed correctly housed the good-time girls that followed the army.

Sol wrinkled his nose. There were the multi smells of horses, their dung and the obnoxious smell of humanity who never washed, pissed and crapped at their convenience, overhung with the stink of burned steaks and bad alcohol.

He stared as he watched a lady

and a young girl step down from a fancy barouche, helped by a soldier in uniform. The woman was stately, hard-faced and richly dressed. The girl looked as if she had stepped straight out of a picture. She was a dainty slim creature with an air of innocence about her.

"God almighty! Just look at them!"

"Yeh, but only look," Paddy said, unimpressed. "That's the colonel's lady and his daughter. There's quite a bunch of white women up there in the fort. It shows it's all quiet at this time. Crazy Horse is away licking his wounds. When the scouts come in with rumours of drums rolling, the first thing they do is evacuate the families. You can always tell the state of the country by the females living in the forts."

"What if the scouts failed to hear the drumbeats?"

Paddy shrugged his wide shoulders.

"It's been known. The womenfolk in Fort St James were all wiped out back in sixty-seven along with the troops.

It's a risky business being married to a soldier."

"Come on, let's get some grub. I can still taste that snake we killed and my guts are killing me. We can bath and change later."

They walked their horses slowly amongst the crowds and except for several cursory glances, no one was interested in them.

They came to a wooden shack from which smells of food came. They dismounted and, hitching their mounts, strode into the dim interior. They blinked from the glare from outside. A short shrunken Chinaman slithered up to them. He grinned widely.

"You come from mines? You want food?"

"Of course. Why do you think we'd come in this stinkhole if we didn't?" The smile disappeared.

"I get food quick," and he slipslopped away behind a sacking curtain and soon an old Chinese woman with no teeth appeared with two plates piled high with steaks and eggs and something that looked like burnt potato. She slammed them down with a frown and held out her hand.

"Ten dollar."

Paddy whistled. "Like hell it is! Two dollars and no more."

"*Ten dollar* or take away!"

Paddy swore and blustered. "That's robbery. I'll not pay . . . " Suddenly there were several Chinese at the old woman's elbow and each held a meat cleaver in his hand and they all looked as if they knew how to use it.

Sol coughed. "I think it would be wise to pay up and look cheerful, especially when you've got you-know-what in your saddle-bags."

The Chinese woman stared at Paddy.

"You men who dig gold, you must pay for your food. We have great difficulty in bringing in cattle for slaughtering. We pay high and so you must pay high."

Paddy sighed and then dug deep into his pocket and brought out the gold.

27

"There you are. Maybe we should bring you a herd of beef and then maybe we should eat free!"

He said this for a laugh but the woman's eyes gleamed.

"You would bring in a herd? Then you certainly would eat free!"

Paddy looked at her and then he looked at Sol and Sol could read his mind. Oh, hell, he thought, here we go again. I only tried nursing cows once and that was enough. Gambling might be hazardous but it's far more comfortable. He waited holding his breath for Paddy's answer.

"Now I might just take you up on that, missus. We've got a little job to do but we could be back."

The woman smiled and Paddy smiled and then he dug into the thick juicy steak and the Chinamen relaxed and went back into the makeshift kitchen.

Sol leaned back and stretched.

"That was good. Never enjoyed a steak so much. Done just right too."

"So you should. I paid for it, remember?"

"Ah shit! Don't be so grumpy. What's ten dollars with what you've got? I thought I was the one who was supposed to be mean!"

Paddy laughed. That was one thing about Paddy. He had a good sense of humour and his tempers didn't last long. They fused and blew and then he was back, the large jolly Irishman singing plaintive songs about home and mothers.

"Let's be away and grab some clothes and then go and find a bath."

They found the same situation in the store. Prices were outrageous, especially spades and hoes and all the things a prospector might need.

They chose the barest of necessities and though Sol grumbled, Paddy was adamant. He wasn't frittering his gold away in luxuries.

So finally when they came to buy their basic commodities there was just flour and salt and coffee and beans and no sugar or tinned peaches or anything to make life a bit easier or pleasant.

"We'll get by on that lot," Paddy growled and he was too big to argue with. Sol shrugged and told himself that he was in a better position than when he'd wandered into Harper's Creek.

"What about liquor?"

"What about it?"

"Don't we take a few bottles with us?"

Paddy thrust his face into Sol's.

"Nope! We have ourselves a drink here in town and then we leave it alone. Right?"

"Er, right, if you say so." But Sol scratched his head and wondered why.

He found out after they'd bathed at the barber's shop and shaved and climbed into their new gear. Sol stared at Paddy. He looked different. He would never have recognized him. He himself felt strange and he smelled different, all yellow soap and no human fat smell.

They walked into the saloon shoulder

to shoulder, the batwing doors swinging viciously behind them. They bellied up to the bar together and the barman took one look and placed two bottles of whiskey before them and two shot glasses.

"Here you are gentlemen. The best in the house."

The barman didn't lie. They'd got the best, probably on account of looking affluent like miners who made good.

A woman in a gaudy red dress trimmed with black lace cosied up to them.

"How about a good time, fellers? I've got a sister upstairs."

"Yeh? Then go and play with her yourself!"

The woman scowled and Sol said hurriedly, "Just a minute, Paddy, aren't you being a little hasty?"

The woman smiled at Sol. "I'm Sadie and my sister's Lucy. Come on fellers, have a good time and relax, or are you impotent, big man?"

Paddy took a swig at the bottle and

half emptied it. He flushed and then brought it down hard on the bartop.

"Impotent? You little bitch! I'll show you whether I'm impotent or not," and he proceeded to tear off Sadie's bodice exposing ripe but saggy breasts. "See what she's offering fellers?" He took a strong grip on the corset below and Sol who had been sitting stupefied, heard the snap of tight laces.

"Paddy, for God's sake!" He could hardly be heard above the screaming and the yelling and cheering of the watching men.

She was down to her drawers when suddenly the nearest men were thrust roughly aside and a great hush descended on the cheering crowd.

Sol looked up at the newcomer in awe. He was taller than Paddy and wide and he had flaming red hair and thick red fuzz covered his arms. He was only wearing trousers and a dirty white vest and the sinews on back and shoulders stood out like cords.

"Let that woman go you son of a

bitch!" The red-haired giant lunged at Paddy and everyone took a step backward.

Sol heard the name Donny McLean whispered like a sigh over the crowd and those that knew Donny quietly left the saloon to wait hopefully outside to see the arrogant Irishman thrown out on his ear.

Inside, the Irishman and the bull-like Scotsman glared eyeball to eyeball like two rams ready to lock horns. With a growl that raised the hairs on those listening and watching, their shovel-like hands grabbed for each other's throats, Sadie being heaved aside in the onslaught.

Sadie landed in a heap on to Sol who hit the floor with a wallop shaking his brains nearly out of his skull. Dimly he heard the racket of the two men swiping at each other while mouthing curses that would curl the toes of ordinary men.

Sol pushed Sadie and her torn petticoats aside, his mind not on warm womanly flesh but on the fight that was threatening to wreck the flimsily built shack.

"Get off me, you stupid bitch! If it wasn't for you, we'd be enjoying a well-earned drink!"

Sol staggered to his feet, ignoring the furious glances from Sadie who now turned her attention to the angry Scotsman.

"Come on, Donny, show the scumbag you mean business. Nobody messes with your woman, right?"

She was yelling and shouting and hopping up and down, her breasts jiggling like a bloodhound's ears.

Sol slapped her mouth.

"Shut it!" he yelled into her ear above the din. "You got what you deserve you old bag! No man or woman insults Paddy Fyngal without paying for it. Now git!"

She got.

Sol was worried. He'd never seen Paddy fight except against himself. This man was even bigger than Paddy and his rage made him twice as strong and wily. The impact of the blows shared made Sol cringe. He could only stand well back and watch helplessly.

But he needn't have worried. Half a bottle of whiskey swilling around in Paddy's guts fixed him into a frenzy. He could have taken on all the Sioux nation.

The end came when a mighty blow from Paddy's right fist lifted Donny McLean high into the air and cracked his head on one of the precarious crossbeams of the saloon. There was an earsplitting crack and the whole of the roof lifted and disintegrated coming down in a roll of rough, unplaned planks on top of those who hadn't been quick enough to tumble out through the batwings.

Sol felt the dull thwack of a plank as it hit him bang on target. He was blacking out when he felt a great hand curl about his new shirt collar and heave him up and over a broad shoulder. Then he was outside being supported by Paddy and watching dazed at the ruin of the front part of the saloon. Only the two-storeyed back side of the building remained along with the wooden staircase leading to the rooms above. Up there were three screaming women in states of undress and a couple of bewildered men still in their long johns and vests.

One man stood scratching his head and looking at the wreckage until a woman came running down the makeshift street, screaming and shaking her fist.

"I'll get you, Willy Fry and I'll cut your balls off when I get you home! That I will!"

Willy Fry, whoever he was, ducked out of sight pretty smartish and once again, Sol thanked his lucky stars he'd never got leg-shackled.

"What do we do now, Paddy?"

"Get out of here, pronto." And they got.

★ ★ ★

They rode until the sun was well down in the sky. Then they found a small stream and some lush grass and made camp. This time they risked a small fire and cooked up beans and made pan bread and they enjoyed it just as much as the Chink's grub. Paddy bathed his cuts and bruises, muttering to himself about wanting a return match with that son of Satan.

"Now, don't go looking for trouble, Paddy. We were lucky to get out before the military came to see what the fuss was about. You know we wanted to keep our heads down and get in and out quick. Now forget that damned feller and go find Stillman and that bloody marshal of yours."

"Aye, you're in the right of it, boyo. 'Tis the whiskey, you see. Makes me fightin' mad and me brains close down and all I want to do is fight. Aye, I'm a rare one when the whiskey gets me. I've broken many a head and never knew it! So, boyo, if you want to keep me out of trouble, don't let me drink whiskey.

I give you the right of it to stop me however you can. Right?"

Sol nodded. He didn't like the idea of being a nursemaid, especially to an Irishman twice the size of himself. Still . . . it was better to have Paddy watching his back than having no one backing him, even if Paddy found trouble as easy as he seemed to.

"If that's what you want."

"That's what I want and if I give you any trouble, hit me over the head. I'll not like it, at all, at all, but I'll forgive you afterwards."

"Hey now, I'm not expecting to have to take the bottle from you by force?" He looked with horror at Paddy. "You are joking, aren't you?"

"Not the divil of a bit of it! If I've already tasted the liquor, I might not want to go along wit' yer. As I say, hit me on the head. That usually quietens me and I'll hold no animosity against you come the morn."

"Bloody hell! What have I got myself into?"

"Oh, we'll get along just foine, boyo," Paddy answered comfortably. "I don't hold grudges and I'm loyal to those who're loyal to me."

With that he burped and farted and scooped a hole in the ground and promptly went to sleep.

Sol lay awake until the first pale streaks of dawn came up over the far mountains. He had a fuller belly than he'd had in months and there was always that tantalizing pair of saddlebags to think and dream about, but why was he so filled with foreboding? Life was exciting with Paddy Fyngal and there was never a dull moment. Then why was he hitching himself about and scratching his arse instead of sleeping?

God damn it all to hell, he muttered and screwed his saddle into a more comfortable position and determinedly shut his eyes to sleep.

The smell of coffee boiling and Paddy's rough hand shaking his shoulder brought him awake in an instant.

He'd been dreaming about having second thoughts about Sadie of the sagging breasts. He'd just gotten a good hold of them while she pulled him close with the promise of the good time to come when he felt someone shoving at his shoulder. Some goddamn two-timer was trying to take her from him. He lashed out and then was catapulted wide awake instantly.

He rubbed his stubbly chin and gazed up at Paddy who grinned.

"Interrupted something, did I? You was groaning fit to bust! I just had to wake you, boyo. I thought you was going to have a heart attack, that I did, boyo."

"You sure pick your time, mister. You could have given me another five minutes." He too grinned. "Anyhow, I always was a loser with women. Me and women are bad luck. I'd rather have a hand of cards!"

He got up, hawked and spat and relieved himself against a rock and then squatted down by the small stream and wetted his head. Now he felt more like tackling Paddy's thick strong coffee. He could smell bacon frying and it set his salivary glands working.

He hunkered down beside Paddy and they shared the meal and Sol felt better.

It was while they shared the last of the coffee that Sol heard the slither of sound. He stiffened, then relaxed and made as if he'd just stretched his back but his quick mind was already assessing the time it would take to roll, seize his gun and fire. He'd already located where the noise had come from.

"What is it?" Paddy's low voice came abruptly.

"Sh! Make as if you haven't noticed a thing."

"I haven't. What in hell's the matter with you?"

"Got thick lugs, eh? Right behind you. When I grab my gun, fling yourself down flat or I'll shoot you through the head."

41

Paddy grunted.

"I hope you know what you're doin' with that there cannon."

"Just watch me!"

Sol waited and watched while he made a cigarette. Then, seeing the bushes before him twitch he grabbed for his gun and yelled and Paddy flung himself sideways and watched fascinated as the weapon seemed to come alive and belch out bullets into the bushes.

There was a yell of pain and then all went quiet and Sol waited and then nodding to Paddy bellied forward and to the right of the bushes while Paddy heaved himself to the left.

They met up behind the bushes where they found the unconscious body of a young Indian. He was a small, slight child of about nine and Sol's bullets, aimed for a grown man's chest, had all but missed him. He had a bullet graze across the top of his scalp which had knocked him out. The boy, whoever he was, would never be so

42

near death again.

Paddy knelt beside him.

"Poor little bugger. You've scalped him, Sol. You're not going to be his favourite person when he wakes up, sure you won't."

"It'll teach him not to sneak up on a body, not from that distance anyway. What'll we do with him? There must be a Sioux camp close by."

The boy opened his eyes while they were cogitating. He looked from one to the other and then the tears came. Paddy put out a gentle hand.

"Hold on there, sonny boy. We're not going to hurt you. You've got a wound that needs dressing." The boy gave a muffled scream and struggled to rise. "Hold on me little tiger." Paddy cursed as the blood ran down the boy's cheek. "Here, Sol, hold him until I find something to soak up this blood."

Sol, not looking happy, gripped the struggling boy in much the same way he'd hold a beaver cub. The boy twisted and tried to bite him and Sol, losing his temper cuffed him soundly.

"There, you ungrateful little devil. You don't know how lucky you are! A bit older, and you would have been up in them hunting grounds, so lie still and let Paddy here cobble you up!"

Paddy set to work. The wound was nasty and would be painful but it wasn't serious. He would have a scar for the rest of his life. Sol watched Paddy at work.

"You've been a doctor, haven't you?"

Paddy stared at him with a sudden blank look in his eyes as if he was transported back to some other time. Then he shook his head and sighed.

"Maybe. What of it?"

"Nothing. It was just the way you handled the boy. If it's something you don't want to talk about . . . "

"I don't particularly. I was in the Union Army. Pressganged as you might say. A general died under my knife. I was accused of being a Confederate spy, would you believe it!"

"And did you murder the general?"

"Never the divil of a bit of it! He would have died under anyone's knife. It was a last ditch try to save him but it didn't work. When they accused me, I hit a major and cut and ran and was hunted for a murderer and a deserter. You see I made the mistake of hitting the general's brother. Out there in the big world, there is a man who would still like to get hold of Paddy Fyngal!"

"And do you think he ever will?"

Paddy shrugged as he tied a kerchief about the boy's brow. "He was a lawyer before he bought into the army; he'll be back East making his gold the easy way. Now boyo, is that comfortable?"

The boy's black eyes travelled over Paddy's face. He nodded.

"You speak English?" Again the boy nodded.

"What's your name?"

"Name, Two Fish."

"Where's your folks? Your lodge? Where is it?"

Two Fish pointed east.

"Long way. White man chase me. I

45

run and hide and run again."

"Then you snuck up to us."

"Smell coffee and food. Hungry."

"Oh, hell! Find this kid something to eat, Sol."

"But . . . "

"Go on, we can do with another brew up. Fry the kid some bacon and make him a flapjack. It's only Christian duty, glory be!"

"Why don't you do it?"

"You're the one who nearly killed the poor little bugger. You do it."

Sol went about the business and soon they were watching Two Fish drinking and digging his strong white teeth into a huge flapjack stuffed with salty bacon.

"What we going to do with him," Sol asked moodily.

"Find his folks and take him home."

"You reckon that's safe?"

"Why not? If my kid was missing I'd welcome the man who brought him home. Indians have feelin's like the rest of us."

"You had many dealings with Indians?"

"Some. Treat 'em right and they treat you right. Very proud are Indians. Don't like being obligated." He laughed. "I'd like to set some of the Indians I've known on to that bloody marshal! Set a fire up his arse all right!"

Sol looked thoughtful. "Maybe this kid may be the means of getting to Black Jack Stillman. As I see it, Indians don't take kindly to folks who dig up the Black Hills."

The boy suddenly took an interest in what was being said.

"Black Jack Stillman? You know this man?"

"Yeh. You've heard of him, Two Fish?" The boy nodded his head vigorously.

"Him bad man. Him talk with fork tongue. He say father kill white men digging ground. Not true."

"You mean Black Jack Stillman is responsible for the miners' deaths?" Paddy turned to Sol. "You're new

47

in these parts. There's been rumours about a band of Indians hiding out in the Black Hills and killing lone prospectors, but if this boyo's telling the truth, then by God, there's goin' to be trouble an' all an' all!"

"But you can't trust this kid's word . . . "

"But he recognized the bastard's name didn't he? He must have heard it from his elders. It makes it more important to go back than ever. It's our Christian duty, boyo, to be sure!"

"Right but we want some back-up. Let's find this kid's folks first and have a parley, unless we get our heads shot off!" Sol was apprehensive. After all, he was the one who'd shot Two Fish and his father might have an impulsive nature.

Paddy looked at Two Fish, noting the drawn face and the pallor, and knew it to be the aftermath of shock.

"You all right, boyo? You can show us where your folks are?"

Two Fish nodded.

"I show you."

"Your pa will not shoot first and ask afterwards when he sees us?"

"I not understand. Why should he do that?"

"Well, he might think you're our prisoner."

The boy laughed and Sol, cautious and suspicious as he was, warmed to him. He was only a kid after all, and an attractive one at that.

"My father is a good and fair man. He only want the right to live free and visit holy places when the time is right. He does not speak with forked tongue like white man."

"How come you speak such good English?"

"Because my father friend of old white man who lives alone in these hills."

"Do you know his name?"

"He calls himself Randel."

"Randel, eh? Now I wonder . . . ?" Paddy scratched his chin and Sol had the feeling Paddy recognized the name.

"Who is he, Paddy?"

Paddy gave a start and looked at Sol as if he'd forgotten his presence.

"Oh! What did you say?"

"I said who is he, this Randel feller?"

"I knew a fair broth of a boy years ago by the name of Jonty Randel. Always fightin' and drinkin' and he could dance and sing with the best of 'em when he was liquored up. I was wonderin' . . ."

"If he was this Randel?"

"Yeh. He killed a man and disappeared. A fight over a woman. Left her behind, that he did. Said he couldn't abide a woman who couldn't play straight with a man. Never heard of him again."

"So you think this feller is him?"

Paddy shrugged.

"Must be plenty of fellers called Randel. He could be anybody so we'll have to wait and see."

"You think we'll meet him?"

"Why not? If he lives near these Indians, we could see him in camp."

"I hope you know what you're

doing," Sol said worriedly. "I feel as if we're walking into a lion's mouth!"

"If you're shit-scared, feller, then stay behind and I'll take him in alone." He looked at Sol contemptuously. "I thought you said you were a gambler!"

"I am, but not with my bloody life! I play cards . . . "

"Oh, don't give me that crap! I saw how you used that gun of yours. You're a quick-on-the-draw shootist and you can't hide the fact when you handle it."

"I can hold my own in a saloon or on the street but Indians . . . the thought of what they can do gives me the creeps."

"Where you been all your life?"

Sol shrugged. "Mainly in the cities and towns and, barring one cattle drive which I found arse-achingly uncomfortable and wouldn't do again, I've bummed around making my living at the tables."

"And not doing it very well, by the state you were in when you hauled me over that cliff."

"Well, we all have our ups and downs. It was a down period and I'm not sure now what period I'm in!"

Paddy grinned. "You can back off, boyo, and go down, or you can stay with me and go on the up. It's your decision."

"Oh, to hell, if you think you can walk into an Indian camp and not shit your trousers, then so can I. After all, I only shot the kid; I didn't kill him!"

So Paddy hoisted the boy up in front of him and led the way by Two Fish's direction and Sol followed.

The way led through tortuous canyons, hot and dim. Screens of trees vied with each other for light as the great jagged teeth of rock rose straight up into the sky. Trickling streams and the flutter of birds disturbed were the only sounds except for their horses' feet as they picked their way slowly along winding paths that could only have been made by wild animals or Indians.

They came to a rocky plateau and far down below a thin blue streak of water echoed the colour of the sky above.

"Now boyo, how do we get to the other side?"

Two Fish grinned.

"There is no need. We are near the lodge. Now we go on foot."

Sol and Paddy looked about them. All was quiet. Nothing stirred, not even a bird.

"I don't believe it!" marvelled Paddy. "There's not a sign of habitation. Nothing."

"Oho!" Sol pointed to a rising peak of rock which looked like a towering needle. "Look over there!" His heart hammered. He could feel the sweat that was on him turn cold, for he was looking up at an Indian standing tall and proud and looking down at them.

Two Fish was waving excitedly, his face alive and joyous.

"It is my brother, Broken Lance. He is looking for me!"

Even as he spoke the Indian slid away into the shadows of the rocks and was gone. Paddy allowed the boy to slide off the horse before alighting himself. Sol followed suit and they hobbled the horses within reach of some good green grass. Then they followed Two Fish along a scarcely discernible trail which gradually descended into a track on the riverbank only feet above the swift-flowing flood.

Then silently and suddenly the Indian was standing before them and he was just as menacing as Sol had imagined. He was a formidable looking figure, well muscled and his bronze skin gleamed. There were two eagle feathers in his headband and he wore an apron made of antelope skin above leather leggings that ended in tough moccasins. In his hand he held an old Spencer rifle and it was aimed at Paddy's heart.

They stopped dead and Two Fish sprang forward, jabbering excitedly. The Indian's look of suspicion softened as he gave the two men a keen glance. Then he patted the boy's head and smiled.

"Two Fish tell me you bring him home. Which one of you shot him?"

Sol coughed.

"Er . . . I did. It was a mistake. I'm sorry."

The Indian nodded.

"I take you both to camp. Our father will want to talk to you. Do you dig for gold?" and now there was a guarded menace in the words.

"No, we're not prospectors."

Broken Lance gave the two men a strange look.

"Then why are you in the Black Hills?"

Sol looked down at his feet and Paddy coughed and smiled ingratiatingly.

"A little bust-up with the law and my good friend here made a bad mistake by tanglin' with Black Jack Stillman."

The Indian's head reared up, anger suffusing his face. Paddy took a step back. "Now, son, don't do anythin' you'll be sorry for!" he said, putting out a hand in instinctive defence.

The Indian, followed by Two Fish,

trotted away and the two men burdened by rifles and Paddy's saddle-bags were hard put to keep up especially as it was new terrain.

The path twisted on itself and passed through tunnels of rock until neither man knew in which direction they were travelling.

Then suddenly they came out into what looked like a shallow bowl surrounded by the jagged peaks of rock. They could hear the sound of water and saw on the right of them a tumbling waterfall which ran into a narrow but deep stream that foamed and swirled. A permanent mist filled the air and so consequently a mass of rank foliage thrived and grew.

It was a beautiful, tranquil place and in the far distance were several tepees. So this was the lodge of this particular band of the Sioux. Broken Lance hesitated and then turned to them and said gravely, "This camp is a temporary one and used only for certain ceremonies. It is most secret and it could mean death for the one who would betray its location whether white or red. Understand?"

"I get your meanin' boyo," Paddy said easily. "But my friend here and me, we believe in hearin' nothin', seein' nothin' and sayin' nothin'. Understand?"

The Indian smiled and nodded and proceeded to trot across the flat grass-covered ground. In the distance they could see a makeshift corral surrounding a bunch of mustangs, hard-muscled beasts but small, bred for the hills and for speed.

As they neared the encampment a small crowd of men, women and children gathered. One woman ran forward with glad cries and snatched up Two Fish and hugged him. A tall man in a war bonnet walked slowly forward, his hand raised in greeting. Broken Lance went and stood before him and their hands met briefly.

Paddy and Sol stood waiting. These moments were vital. Sol risked a few whispered words.

"I want to shit!"

"Hang on, dummy, or we'll lose face! Appear frightened and they'll think we're lying and that we're looking for gold."

"What about that gold in your saddle-bags?"

"They're not interested in minted gold. It's the rough stuff out of their beloved hills they're worried about."

"Oh hell . . ."

"What's up?"

"I think I'm going to . . ."

"Stop it! Think of the last woman you were with!"

Sol groaned.

"I don't think it's going to make any difference!"

"Jesus, you must be in a bad way!"

Suddenly the two Indians turned to look at the two white men. Sol jumped and nipped his arse tight. This was the moment of truth and he wasn't going to die a craven, shit-legged coward.

Then the truth dawned on him.

The two Indians were smiling and the relief was nearly a disaster. Still, he hung on.

"My father was angry that I brought two strangers to this camp but when I told him the reason and gave him the assurance that this place would never be revealed by you, he now welcomes you to his tepee. You will come with us, please."

Sol gave Paddy an agonized look which Paddy interpreted rightly.

"Er, before we start the pow-wow, Broken Lance, could we . . . relieve ourselves? It's been a long trek."

The Indian smiled with amusement.

"Certainly." He spoke to his father whose stern craggy face split into a wicked grin. He spoke fast.

"My father says you may enter the cave of snakes and do what you have to do. We do not allow pollution on the open ground." He led the way to an outcrop of boulders and gestured at an entrance to a cave that was only big enough for them to crawl through.

"You mean we're to crawl in there, and there's snakes?" Sol squeaked.

Broken Lance nodded gravely.

"A man isn't a man if he cannot face the unknown with bravery and distinction." He put a hand inside the hole and brought out a short stubby branch which was coated with resin and covered in dried grass. This he lit with a flint and steel from a pouch he wore. Sol watched fascinated. Then when it was well alight, Broken Lance handed it to Sol.

"You look in the most need."

Sol swallowed and took the burning brand and crouching low steeled himself to creep inside. At first the smoke dipped and swirled and he coughed but then it flared and he saw the cave was bigger than it appeared from the outside. The floor was of soft sand and as he came upright he saw that it was domed like a church overhead.

But where were the snakes? He'd visualised them to be covering the ground in a writhing mass. There were none and he felt weak with relief. Then he saw the pit and walked to it, drawn by the smell and he knew this was the place he had to use. He saw the overhanging slab of rock and knew this was the place he must make for.

He balanced the burning brand in the crack of two split rocks and then did what he was aching to do. The physical relief was instantaneous. He could have cried.

Then as he stood up and pulled up his trousers he heard the menacing hiss and stared down into the black void below him. He could dimly see the movement far below. So that was where the snakes lived!

Then taking the smoking torch he made his way back to the entrance and it was then he saw the crude pictures painted in ochre and red and black of snakes of all kinds with bizarre stripes on elongated bodies.

He laughed in relief. This was a holy place in honour of snakes. Broken

Lance hadn't been about to kill him in some subtle way!

He emerged from the hole, grinning. Paddy looked at him in wonder.

"You all right, boyo?"

"Yeh, go on, get yourself inside. It's quite an experience."

Paddy looked at him narrowly.

"I think my bladder will wait."

"Suit yourself," and Sol grinned at Broken Lance who grinned back.

They got a surprise when they entered the chief's tepee. It wasn't going to be a nice cosy little chitchat. There were five figures sitting quietly well away from the flames of a small fire that smouldered on a blackened hearthstone. The air in the tepee smelled of unwashed bodies, pipesmoke and the scent of pine needles that spluttered on the fire.

Broken Lance introduced the two men and then said softly. "This is my father, Hunting Bear, and these are our good friends, Randel, Parker and the brothers, Jordache."

Behind them one of Hunting Bear's women attached a burning brand to one of the uprights of the tepee. It smouldered but gave off enough light for them to see the strangers.

Paddy laughed and stepped forward. "Holy mother of God! It is Jonty Randel. How are you, boyo? Don't you remember, Paddy Fyngal?"

3

HUNTING BEAR sat quietly watching the newcomers greeting the white men behind him. He nodded imperceptibly to his son who withdrew from the tepee leaving the men alone. Motioning with his hand, the two men sat down cross-legged before him.

"My son tells me the shooting of the boy was an accident. He was foolish to come so close but the boy has no experience and he was frightened and hungry. But that is no excuse. He moved like a buffalo and must bear the consequences. It will teach him to move in silence. Broken Lance also tells me you have Black Jack Stillman as your enemy. Is that right?"

Sol cleared his throat.

"I was run out of Harper's Creek for trying to steal some of his gold, then he set his hound on to me. I owe him no favours."

Paddy grinned.

"Black Jack is no friend of mine either. He's got the marshal of Harper's Creek in his pocket along with the official gold assayer. He's got a good thing going in them there Black Hills. Lets the miners stake their claims and dig for the yaller stuff and when there's a lucky strike Black Jack moves in with his gunnies and either frightens the poor bastard away or kills him. He don't mind which. Then he takes over the claim and everybody plays blind and deaf and dumb."

Hunting Bear nodded.

"It is said that the Sioux kill these lone miners but it is not so. We object to the desecration of our holy places and we protest but we do not kill as the white men allege. We are willing to live by the law of the white man as long as the miners stay within the limits that your government have ruled to be mined. But Black Jack Stillman's men trespassed into our designated areas and must be stopped. We are a small band and have not the means to fight this Stillman and his hired gunmen."

"So what do you want us to do?" Paddy Fyngal glanced at the silent Jonty Randel and the other white men.

Hunting Bear smiled but there was no amusement in his eyes.

"Kill Black Jack Stillman and rid the Hills of this canker that lurks everywhere."

Jonty Randel got awkwardly to his feet. He was a broad, squat man with long grey hair and dressed in the skins of a hunter. Paddy saw that one leg was twisted and he moved with an odd lurching gait. He came and stood in the middle of the tent and the fire showed up the gaunt face and Sol, seeing him for the first time, gasped. If he wasn't mistaken this man had been tortured nearly to the death.

Sol glanced at Paddy and saw the shock on his face. Then as his eyes

66

became accustomed to the gloom he looked hard at the other men who'd been introduced as Parker and the three Jordache brothers. His blood ran cold as he realized that all the men had been tortured. Jeese! Sol felt the return of his loose bowels. Had they been tortured by Indians or had it been Stillman and his friends? The answer soon came.

Jonty Randel looked at his friends and then directly at Paddy Fyngal.

"We're the only survivors of a mining camp that was called Schmid's Gully. There was a bunch of us working together and we hit it big. Carl Schmid was the only experienced gold-digger but the claim was so rich, he reckoned that all us twenty-one men would be dollar millionaires in two years. But the first time we hauled in our gold to Harper's Creek and the assay report was proven, then we were in trouble. When we started work again and all present, they came down from the hills and surrounded us and for them it was like killing jack-rabbits. Some of our fellers didn't even know how to shoot a gun never mind own one. It was a massacre. We're only alive because we were the ones who took that gold into Harper's Creek and they were convinced we had a cache hidden away." Jonty Randel sighed. "You can see they tortured us all. They even tore out Willy's tongue to make his brothers talk. But it was no use. We had no gold. We'd spent what that first lot was worth on supplies. So they shot us and threw us into a crevice of rock. We owe our lives to Parker. He'd gone to piss and he hid until they'd gone and then he dragged us out of that chasm and nursed us all until Hunting Bear happened along and brought us into camp."

"And you've been here ever since?"

"Yeh. It's taken a long time to recover. So will you help us?"

Paddy scratched his chin and looked at Sol.

"What do you think, boyo?"

Sol shrugged in typical Jewish fashion.

"What can we do? Your mine must have made him a rich man. He can hire all the bullyboys he needs to clean this whole camp out."

"But there's all the miners. All they need is a good leader."

"But what about a plan?"

"Oh, we've got a plan. All we need are two good men to lead and carry it out."

"But what about you, Jonty?"

Jonty Randel laughed bitterly. Looking down at his leg he said quietly, "I'd make a good leader, wouldn't I, with this gammy leg? But I would have a part to play. I could keep watch and signal, if you would use my plan. God knows I've had long enough to perfect it!"

Paddy grunted. He looked at the Indians.

"Are the Sioux part of your plan?"

"No. That's why I'd rather keep this in the miners' hands and then the Indians aren't implicated. There's been too much blame attached to the Indians."

"Have you talked to the miners?"

"Some. There's a growing resentment amongst them and yet none dares to stand up to Stillman and his crew. Many of the miners have upped stakes and left of their own accord and anyone taking over the claims has had to answer to Stillman. He's either for him or against him and if he's against, then an accident happens."

"Huh! Maybe Sol and me might go right in there and lay claim to one of the abandoned mines. He knows Sol and so he'll come after us."

"Now wait a minute . . . " Sol didn't like Paddy's hotheaded idea of barging in, regardless. "Let's hear Randel's plan first."

"You willing to listen, Fyngal?"

"Yeh, get on with it. It's the only way we'll get cautious Sol here to co-operate."

Sol flushed angrily. "I'm not a fighting man, Paddy but I'm not yeller. It's just I like to use my brains about these things and not rush in like a fool . . . "

"You mean I'm a fool?" Paddy's voice was very quiet.

"Not a fool, just an Irish hothead. You'll fight for the love of it and talk afterwards. Now me, I like to know exactly what I'm getting into. Anything wrong in that?"

"Well, if you put it like that . . . "

"Do you want to hear the plan or not?" and now it was Randel who was getting impatient.

"Go ahead, boyo. If we don't like it, we'll tell you, sure as eggs have to be cracked to make an omelette!"

The two Indians looked a little puzzled.

"What's this about eggs?" asked Hunting Bear.

"Jesus!" Randel swore. "Just let me tell you my plan before I burst!"

"Go on then. I don't know what's stopping you!" Paddy grinned at Randel's exasperation.

71

"Well, it's like this. Stillman always waits until the miners bring in their gold before he pounces. He's got the assayer and the marshal under his thumb and so when the assayer gives the marshal the wink, then the marshal sends word to Stillman and he comes running with his boys."

"Yeh, I gathered something of the kind. Then what?"

"He comes down hard on the miner in question. He usually waits until the feller has his paydirt and they highjack him after he's had a few nights on the razzle in the town. Or if the feller reckons to want to put his paydirt straight into the bank and there's enough of it, there's a bank raid. Savvy? He's got his men lined up for their different jobs. Sometimes a feller loses his dust before he even gets it to the assayer if he gambles. It's been known and there's many a man been shot down either in the saloon or out in one of the lanes at the back. He doesn't always use the same tricks, but all the crime harks back to him and his boys."

"Then how do we come in?"

"We send the word around to the miners we know to hold on to their dust and cache it and they will pass on the word to the others. If there's no gold being taken in to be assayed, then Stillman and the rest are going to panic. He'll send his men out to sniff around and find out what's happening."

"Then what?"

"Why, we send out the rumours of a big cache waiting for a government bigwig who is offering a higher price and a guarantee of safety for the despatching."

"That will get Stillman in a tizz! But haven't you forgotten something?"

"What? I think I've thought of everything."

"He'll not believe there's a government assayer coming unless the Harper Creek telegrapher can confirm it."

"I know Cal Graham. He's an honest man. A word to him and he'll get one of his buddies down the line to send a message. Oh yes, I'd thought of that."

Paddy nodded approvingly.

"Do we really have a cache?"

"Oh, yes. There'll be a cache but that is one of the things we've got to decide, just where and when."

Paddy grinned. "I can tell you where if you say when."

Randel looked at him with surprise.

"You don't know this country."

"Maybe not but I know an ideal place for a cache and more importantly it would be safe."

"You're joking. It sounds too good to be true!"

Paddy rasped his chin in the way Sol was coming to recognize as his way of hiding the fact that his brains were whizzing around like clockwork wheels. He had something up his sleeve all right!

"You remember the military payroll that went missing? The one on its way to Fort Laramie?"

"Yes. I remember it. Disappeared and no trace after the massacre."

"Well, I was one of the guards and I was one who helped to stash it. The others were killed."

"You mean . . . ?" and all the men listening, tensed, waiting for Paddy's answer.

"Yeh, most of it's still there in all its glory, my boyo. What do you think of that?"

Jonty Randel licked his lips.

"I'd like to get my hands on it!"

"I bet you would! So would the military and they've sent out many a detail to hunt for the stuff and gone back empty-handed."

"You would give up the secret location to help us?"

"At a price."

"What would that be?"

"That all the gold was shipped out under guard and I would have sole authority to how it should be doled out. There's plenty for all of us." Paddy looked around at the watching men. "If you help me, I'll help you!"

"And what do you *really* want, Paddy Fyngal? It's not just about getting gold out, is it? There's something else?"

Paddy Fyngal's face hardened.

"You don't have to know my business, Randel. As far as you're concerned, boyo, you'll get the help you need to smash Stillman and his gold consortium, and we all prosper in the process. I'm sure not one of you can quibble at that?" He looked around at the other men. "You all want to be rich, don't you? I tell you there's enough stashed away for us all!"

Sol looked at Paddy and wondered. Until now he'd just thought of him as an Irishman who could lay his hands on a military payroll when he was short of cash. Now he wondered what lay behind the façade of Irish wit and geniality.

One thing was sure: it was something mighty serious for him to give away the secret of that cache and to offer to share it between them all, yes, mighty serious.

Randel went into a huddle with his men and Sol noticed he did the talking and the men did the head shaking. Then he was back.

"We'll go along with what you want," he said briefly to Fyngal. "What's on your mind?"

"We help you break Stillman and his scum and in return you help us to break into Fort Laramie!"

Sol was stunned, as was Randel and the listening men. Someone laughed and Fyngal looked grim.

"This is no laughing matter. I'm being damned serious, and there's a good reason which you don't need to know at this stage. Are you on?"

Randel nodded slowly.

"Your explanation's going to have to be good, Fyngal, but I'll go along with it for now and so will the boys. But one thing's clear: we want to know the why and wherefore before we put our heads in the lion's mouth."

"That figures. I'd feel the same way myself. But the fact of the matter is that what I've got in mind could be blown by careless talk."

Randel bristled. "I know these boys through and through. They're loyal and . . . "

"Goddammit! I'm not thinking of present company!" Fyngal interrupted impatiently. "If we're to involve the miners and Stillman brings in the military as I think he might, then one wrong word could send the balloon up!"

Ned Parker moved uneasily and looked at Randel for guidance, then said quietly, "You think Stillman will bring in the military? That would be war."

"I don't think, buster, I *know*! How many gunnies has he got? twenty . . . thirty? So if the miners revolt, it could mean a couple of thousand men. He'd have to call in the military, unless we get the first shots in and cripple him good and proper."

"How would we do that?"

Fyngal looked round at the watching men.

"By infiltrating his mines and blowing the buggers up at the same time."

There was a long intake of breath and then Jonty Randel laughed and broke the spell.

"Are you in your right mind? Stillman owns half the mines in these hills. We'd never do it."

"Why not?"

"Well, there's the explosives for one thing."

"The miners have explosives. They can arrange amongst themselves who does what. It's a matter of getting the best men together and selling them the idea."

"But what about the bastards who take Stillman's judas money. There's a lot of lickarses about."

"They must make sure they have 'em sewn up on the night. It can be done."

"But what about Stillman and his

brother-in-law and the assayer, Bill Tomlin?"

"You can leave them to us!" Cas Jordache butted in, his scarred face grim and relentless. "We owe him for what he did to us." He looked across at Willie who sat morose with head down and a glazed look in his eyes."

"So? We'll give it a try?"

Fyngal looked round at the others. They nodded except for Willie who looked as if he was in another place.

There was an interruption. Hunting Bear coughed and signalled to his wife hovering in the opening of the tepee. She went outside and Broken Lance stooped and entered, his black eyes flashing from one to each of them.

"You want me, Father?"

"Yes, my son. You will listen to the plans to overthrow the white man with the black heart. You will go with them and find the one called Big Nose who scouts for the military. You will bring him here and we shall talk."

Broken Lance nodded and sat down

behind his father and waited.

"This Big Nose, who is he?" Fyngal looked from the chief to Randel.

"He's a scout and he comes and goes at will. He is very useful to us, for he knows everything. Mind you, the chief trusts him more than I do," Randel said softly but the chief's eyes flashed. He might be old but his ears were keen, and Sol, watching and listening, decided that no matter how friendly the old man was, he was still an Indian, to be watched.

Sol dozed a little while the men talked and made plans. He was a virtual stranger in these parts and so he was in no position to advise or comment. He would go along with what his new friend Fyngal wanted to do.

But later, when they were settling down in a small tepee put at their disposal, Sol asked the questions he'd been wanting to ask for the last six hours.

"Paddy, how come you want to get

into the fort? Why didn't you do what you wanted to do when we were there earlier?"

Fyngal's smile was enigmatic.

"I was using my eyes and listening to the gossip as well as enjoyin' that itsy-bitsy trouble we were after havin'."

"But why for heaven's sake?"

"Aye, but you're like a rat, boyo, gnawing away and bitin' and tearin' to get at the meat on the bone! But there, if you're with me, you've got the right of it to know and bless me, I think you can keep that big Jew mouth of yours tight shut! Now I can rely on you, boyo?"

"Of course you can! You know me . . . "

"But that's it, boyo, I *don't* know you. Sure, we're pards and for the time we've been together, I trust you, up to a point bearing in mind the gold . . . for gold can be the very divil and makes for loose tongues. So, in the long term, can you be trusted?" Sol spat in disgust.

"Jesus! I can hardly fathom your reasoning, Paddy. You either trust me or you don't!"

Sol was feeling his temper rising. What did the bastard want?

"Oh, very well, I'll trust you, but mind you, if you let me down, I'll scalp you, see if I don't!"

"Aw to hell! I'm not that interested anyway. But for the life of me I can't see you as a doctor cutting off generals' legs and being a bloody guard looking after a payroll! It doesn't make sense and for why you should be interested in the fort . . . aw hell, keep your secrets to yourself!" He gave an exaggerated shrug of the shoulders. Fyngal grinned.

"Your head nearly disappeared. That shrug tells the world you're a Jew."

"What of it? I'm proud to be a Jew. Now just leave me alone. I should have known better than to think you might treat me like a real pard!"

"Hey now, you are a real pard!"

"Then why don't you just come clean?"

Fyngal sighed. "I'm not a man who opens his heart easy. There's sore places inside of me and things I don't like to think about. I'm just a soft, easy-goin' Irish mick when I gets down to it. It's the grievin' heart of me that keeps it all back . . ."

"Oh, Paddy, have you been drinking?"

"Niver a divil of a bit of it! I assure you, Sol of the hard unbelieving heart, that I'm just a hurtin' and lonely man . . ." His voice quivered and Sol watched him open-mouthed. This was some crazy man, of mixed up emotions. Then as he watched, he saw the gleam of something else in Paddy's eyes. "But I'm a man of vengeance too!" he roared, and shook his fist in the air.

Sol took a step backwards. This was more like the Paddy he knew.

"Come on then, Paddy, unburden yourself. I'm your pard, remember?"

The moment of self pity was gone. Paddy flung himself down on his makeshift bed and then said in a tired voice, "You'll have to know. I might as well tell you now as later. I was a doctor. I was drafted into General Rosecrans' army and was at the battle of Chattanooga. It was hell." Paddy paused and Sol saw he was reliving those harsh nightmarish days of makeshift hospitals and stench-laden shacks he'd worked in. "Then Rosecrans was relieved of his command after the Battle of Chickamauga. It was chaos; bodies everywhere and men dying through disease and the filth of rotting bodies and bad weather. General Conrad had no sooner taken over than he was shot in the leg by a sniper. We were all tired and drunk with fatigue. Some of the medics had worked for forty-eight hours at a stretch, I amongst them. I didn't see the general for the first two days and when I did, I saw he was going to die of lead poisoning if I didn't do something about it. So, I took his leg off. We had no laudanum, only whiskey, and he was raving when I finally operated. His heart couldn't stand the strain. He died before we could bandage up his stump. That was when the trouble started."

"How was that?" Sol spoke cautiously. He could see the sudden emotion welling up in the man and it was nothing to do with a general's leg being hacked off or his death.

"He had a brother, Major Dwight B. Conrad and the B stood for bastard. He blamed me for the general's death. Accused me of being a spy and deliberately botchin' the job, begod! He called me a butcher! Me! Who'd saved countless lives in that bloody battle! I wouldn't take it. I trounced him good and proper!"

"You struck an officer?"

"Yeh, and I enjoyed the doin' of it! It felt good, but he had me put in irons, the murderin' bastard . . . " Paddy's face set and a tear trickled down his cheeks. "He took my brother . . . "

"You had a brother?"

"Yeh. Liam. I'd promised Ma to look out for him. He was a few cents less than a dollar, you understand, but he was a good man, strong and docile and he followed me like a dog. He was the best nursing medic in my team, that he was, God rest his soul! He was a lovely brother, was our Liam."

"Then what happened to him?"

Paddy was silent for a long time and then he said quietly, "That bastard of a major had him tied down on one of our makeshift operating tables and he sliced Liam's leg off with his sword!"

Sol listened with horror, his guts churning.

"You mean he deliberately and cold-bloodedly chopped off your brother's leg for no reason?"

"Oh, he thought he had a reason, all right. It was my brother for his brother. Liam died too for loss of blood. That was the night I deserted. One of my medics cut me free and I got away, intending to come back and slit the bastard's throat. But the very next morning Major Dwight Conrad was called to Washington and he got away."

"That was when you joined up again as a private?"

"Yeh, after a few months. I figured it was the only way to catch up with him. But I never did, until now, that is."

"You mean he's stationed in Fort Laramie?"

Paddy grinned and Sol saw a hint of madness in the blue Irish eyes.

"Yeh. He and his wife and daughter," and Paddy licked his lips.

"Are they why you want to break into Fort Laramie?" Nameless horrors filled Sol's mind. Was it chopping off legs, or rape or some other kind of torture that Paddy had in mind?

Paddy looked at him sharply. He had an animal's instinct when it came to a man's reactions.

"You don't approve?"

"I don't approve of bringing a man's family into a personal feud. What good would it do?"

"If a man had to choose between his

wife and his daughter, it would cause some emotional stress even in such a man as Major Conrad, wouldn't you think?"

"What would you do?"

"Take off a leg, what else?"

"Then you would be as big a bastard as the major. You would come down to his level." Sol turned away in disgust.

Paddy looked at his back, considering.

"There could be other ways . . . "

Sol turned swiftly. "I knew you would see reason. Just concentrate on the major!"

4

BLACK JACK STILLMAN looked at the two men. They were in Bill Tomlin's office next door to the bank in Harper's Creek. Both men looked worried for Jack Stillman wasn't noted for his patience and forbearance even with his own men. They expected an eruption and they got it.

"What the hell is going on? Not one ounce of dust or a nugget for a whole week? There's something afoot or the bloody Black Hills is running out of gold! Or are you two playing funny buggers with me?" He caught Bill Tomlin by the collar and pulled him close. "Are you, by God?" and he shook the wretched man.

Bill Tomlin choked and thrashed feebly and Jed Payne grabbed Stillman's arm.

"Hold on, Jack. It's not what you

think. There's no doublecross. Why should we muck up a perfectly good set-up?"

Jack Stillman paused and then threw the smaller man aside and Bill Tomlin clutched his throat and coughed and then gasped for breath, carefully avoiding Stillman's eyes for at that moment if he'd been big enough and strong enough he would have killed the bastard. Hatred filled him like a canker but Stillman held his job on the line. One complaint from Jack and his job with the Gold Corporation would go down the pan and he couldn't afford that.

"By God, if you're fooling me, Jed, I'll have the balls off you both and to hell with Mary even though she's my sister."

"I've told you, it's nothing to do with us. It's just . . . just one of those things!" But he knew it wasn't and he was uneasy. The mines had been quiet for a week, no drunkenness and no fights and everyone being matey and friendly. It didn't smell right. Even Jock Macduff and Taffy Llewellyn had made up their racial differences and were drinking together all mellow and palsy-walsy. He couldn't understand it but it smelled trouble.

He hadn't been able to arrest a feller for pissing against a wall. It was eerie and the marshal's office was down on fines. There wasn't enough in the kitty to pay his wages never mind his deputy's.

He had enough to worry about, never mind coping with his foul-tempered brother-in-law.

"Well? What's the answer, Jed? Why are the miners ganging together and not bringing in their gold?"

"I don't know, Jack. Have you heard any whispers, Bill?"

The small, painfully gaunt Bill Tomlin licked his lips and looked anywhere but at Jack Stillman.

"There's a rumour going around that someone's organizing them into some kind of army."

"Why the hell didn't you send word to me out at the ranch? I would have come in and stamped out all this nonsense. Now it might be too late."

"Look, Mister Stillman, the miners usually bring in their ore on a weekend when they come into town for supplies. Some don't even come in weekly. They come in when they want supplies, those that have their diggings well away from town. How should I know what is going on?"

"You should keep your ear to the ground! God knows, you get a good rip-off. You can afford to pay regular wages to your spies. I've told you both time and time again you must know every detail that goes on in this town! You're fools the pair of you!"

"That's not fair, Mister Stillman . . . "

"Not fair? Have I to do all the thinking for you? I set the arrangement up. Must I wipe your arses for you? Do you want the cash without even working for it? Do you? Do you?"

"Now steady on, Jack. We'll get

the situation under control. They're bound to bring in some gold by next weekend. Those fellers will want cash for food and women. It's just natural. And they'll be a thirsty lot to boot."

"Then we'll have to make sure that prices rise. Tell that fool of a storekeeper that no one buys a thing on tick and he wants gold instead of dollars and the same to the saloonkeepers. They've got to take gold not dollars."

"But . . . "

"No buts, Jed. They can't refuse. I've got all their IOU notes stitched up at the bank. They'll co-operate. In the meanwhile I'll get my men lined up and give the miners a lesson in co-operation!"

Jack Stillman swung out of the assayer's office like a hurricane, leaving Jed Payne and Bill Tomlin looking at each other.

"What will he do when he hears that Paddy Fyngal is behind all this trouble?"

"Maybe we should have told him," Bill Tomlin said nervously, fingering his bruised throat.

"He'll find out soon enough," Jed Payne said, with much feeling. "I'd rather be miles away when he erupts. Let someone else take the flak for a change."

Black Jack stood outside and lit a long cigar. He was a fine figure of a man, six foot three in his socks and broad with it. He was a muscular man, his shoulders betraying the fact that in his younger days he'd been no mean wrestler. Now going on fifty, he was satisfied with being the power in the Black Hills. The feeling of power was better than winning a fight any day. He was now pitting his wits against all men and he was winning hands down.

He surveyed the long straggly street that was Harper's Creek. He owned most of it and as it was growing rapidly, he was becoming a very rich man.

He had a dream and it was fast

coming to fruition. He saw himself as an up and coming politician and his goal was the senate itself. He was a good speaker and he had no delusions of what he would become. He was on the way to the top and no one was going to stop him.

He decided that he would go and visit Jeanie, the latest imported whore from New York. She was different to the other sleazy women who followed the miners. For one thing Jeanie bathed herself in her imported hip-bath and sometimes invited himself to share it. It was marvellous what Jeanie could get up to in that bath . . .

She soothed his nerves and flattered him. He needed her now. He had a lot to think about.

She was a pretty creature with long blonde hair which she swept upwards and coiled on the top of her head with wisps of curls left loose at the sides. She wore pretty, impractical dresses, left over from her more affluent days in New York. She didn't look like a girl who would stick a knife into a punter, but she had done just that back in New York. Miss Jeanie Gleeson was a wanted woman back East, for putting out the lights of a very influential man who'd been a friend of the mayor of New York.

Black Jack wasn't aware of Jeanie's past or her steely strength of character. He just knew her as a woman who catered well for his needs. He had no idea she could threaten and carry out her threats. Jeanie wasn't the woman to be intimidated by any man.

She was surprised to see him. Five minutes earlier and he would have had evidence that she didn't exactly go by his rules, insofar as she was supposed to be his exclusively.

Jeanie liked a change. It wasn't her style to remain faithful to anyone even if they had the cash to buy her. Black Jack's body wasn't the kind to thrill her. She liked young, lithe bodies which could surprise her into real moans of ecstasy. Black Jack was hard work and she had to do all the running while he lay back and closed his eyes and enjoyed it. It wasn't fair and if it wasn't for his generosity, and she couldn't fault him for that, but he insisted on value for money . . . she would have shown him the door long ago.

Now she faced him in a pretty, blue, filmy gown that matched her eyes. Her hair hung low over her shoulders framing her face. She looked like an angel.

Black Jack frowned when he saw her.

"You had a visitor?"

Her eyes opened wide. She looked the picture of hurt innocence. "Jack, you don't think I'd two-time you?" thanking God that Phil Jobling, the son of the banker, had got clean away. "I've been catching up on my beauty sleep. You don't want a wrinkled hag to come to?" She smiled winsomely and stroked his cheek. His eyes softened and his voice thickened. He pushed the unruly hair from her eyes. "You look beautiful with your hair loose," and he bent to kiss her.

She stood quite still while he took her lips. He was much taller than she was and she feared him. His dark swarthy looks and his broad shoulders and big stomach reminded her of a rampant bull. He had never actually hit her but she felt instinctively that his inner violence was very near the surface. She'd seen how he dealt with those who angered him. She knew she would not be exempt from his anger if she annoyed him. Now she stood quietly while he pawed her. She stiffened instinctively when his hand moved up her thigh, and he was aware of it. He frowned.

"Come on, make it hot. Don't stand there like a frozen statue. Get to work. What do I pay you for?"

She flushed. She was a whore and a good one at that, but she had her pride. She didn't like the fact pushed down her throat and just lately he'd taken it upon himself to remind her of what she was and that he owned her, just because he paid her bills.

"Jack, I'm not in the mood. I've got a headache."

Jack Stillman caught her by the wrist and twisted her arm. She yelped, wondering what had made him in such a temper.

"You'll do as I say, headache or no headache and I want it *now!*" He yanked her arm and this time she screamed in agony. Then he thrust her on to the bed and tore the flimsy robe from her, exposing her quivering body.

"Now get to work!"

She was no stranger to brutality. There'd been many men in her life who'd treated her like some animal on which to take out their lust. Now she did what she'd done many times before, she closed her mind to who she was with or what she was doing and went in to automatic response.

But Jack Stillman wasn't easily satisfied and she was trembling when finally he rolled away from her sweating and appeased.

Then he got up abruptly and adjusted his clothing.

"You're slipping, old girl. You'll have to do better than that or you're out on your ear. Maybe it's time I brought in a nice fresh young girl."

Jeanie's eyes smouldered as she reached for a shawl to cover herself. So he thought she was over the hill, eh? She would show him! Some time, some place, he would let his guard down and she would trample his face in the dust!

She smiled automatically although her body ached and she yearned for a bath to clear his stink away.

"Young ones might be fresh but they haven't the expertise we more mature women have," she said pleasantly.

He snorted. "You didn't show much expertise just now," he snarled. "You'd better get your act together tonight, or I'll be wanting to know the reason why.

You sure you haven't had a man up here?"

Her temper rose. She was in mind to be reckless, and then caution gripped her throat.

"I've told you, I've been resting. I'm not a machine, you know."

He grunted and reached for his hat and the relief in her was tremendous when he finally opened the door and left.

She tucked the hundred dollars he'd thrown contemptuously at her into a black tin box which held a thick wad of notes and gold. When she had enough she was going as far away from Harper's Creek and that filthy bastard as was possible to go. It had been a mistake listening to his lies back in New York that she would step into a freer happier life. She was more of a prisoner here in these backwoods than ever she would have been in a brothel. Now all she could think of was to get out.

She called the odd job boy who

did the dirty jobs in the hotel where Stillman rented her rooms and he brought up hot water again and she soaked her abused body.

Downstairs, Jack Stillman questioned the hotelkeeper before speaking to the barman. Neither had seen any man going upstairs to Jeanie's rooms. He was only half satisfied. He knew she was more popular than he was in this community. Both men could be lying. If he ever found out they were, he'd have 'em both skinned alive.

He took the free bottle of whiskey offered by the barman and took a long swig and then tucked the bottle into the capacious pocket in the long black coat he favoured. He looked like a senator or a respectable lawman and he cultivated this image. It made him feel good and enhanced his power.

Several men nodded to him in the street but a few acquaintances shied away from him. He frowned. He could smell insubordination. It was time to bring in his bullyboys and teach the town a lesson. It wasn't only the miners who were revolting, it was the tradesmen too.

Jack Stillman's temper simmered to boiling point. A wrong word or a careless glance and mayhem would break out. A couple of hours with the sweating Jeanie hadn't taken the edge off him. That was another thing that worried him. It was getting harder to get it up and keep it up. It must be Jeanie's fault, not his. But a little voice inside him niggled. Was there something wrong with him? But he pushed that thought away. Of course it was Jeanie to blame. It had to be!

He slammed back the batwing doors of the seediest saloon in town. It was not much more than a soddy with sagging roof and a couple of planks for a bar. Behind the bar was a squat, round-bellied man who resembled the beer casks lined up behind him.

His eyes flickered when he saw who was standing there. Jack Stillman never visited him in his own saloon. The rule was, a discreet message and Sam Tossil would wait until the last of the town revellers had hit the sack and then he would go and report to Jack under cover of darkness. There was no man alive who knew Sam's business with Jack Stillman.

Now, Sam looked carefully around the filthy drinking den. The air was blue with smoke and foul to the nose. Apart from four men arguing in one corner and a drunk with his head on his hands on his bartop, the place was empty. Sam vaguely wondered about the drunk.

Swiftly he moved his bulk forward and lifted the man's chin. The eyes opened vaguely. Sam knew the signs. This feller was not feigning drunkenness. He would be out for at least twelve hours, but to make certain he picked him up and threw him over his shoulder and strode out to the back without a word to Stillman and deposited the drunken man amongst a mound of rotting garbage.

Then without a change of expression he was back.

"What will you have, Mister Stillman?"

Stillman pulled a face.

"What have you got besides that muck you sell in the barrels?"

"I've got a bottle of real whiskey."

"Then why ask me what'll I have? Bring it out."

"Was it wise to come here, Mister Stillman?"

"Look, don't you ask me if I'm wise or not! I know what I'm doing. Now what's your story about these bloody miners? You must have heard rumours."

"That's just it, Mister Stillman. There's no rumours. The men are playing a tight game. If I'd heard anything for definite, I should have sent you word. But there's nothing to tell. Trade's dead. You can see for yourself. They're all out there working their butts off and not even coming in for a drink. It's unnatural and I don't like it, but what can I do?"

"What about your girls? Aren't they working?"

"Not a bit of it. Some of 'em are talking about pulling up stakes and getting out. If one goes, they'll all go and then where will we be? A town without women." He spat on the dirt floor and rubbed it with the toe of his boot. "Chre-ist! What will folks think if we can't keep our girls in work?"

"They'll think you're all a bunch of puffs!" Sam laughed nervously, although he didn't think it very funny. But Stillman roared his disapproval.

"It's no laughing matter, Sam. Goddammit! If we get a bad reputation we'll have all the scumbags in creation coming down on us like bees to a honeypot!"

"But I thought . . . " stammered Sam, now bewildered.

"Don't think, just listen and find out what I want to know. Savvy!"

Sam nodded his head violently, taking a peek at the four men in the corner. The bastards were not talking but listening and Sam knew they knew him for what he was . . . an informer. He might as well pack his bags and get out of town. It was a miserable place anyway. He would be glad to leave. He spat on the ground.

"I savvy, Mister Stillman. I'll do what I have to do. You can depend on that." He grinned and watched Stillman take another swig at the bottle. By cripes! He could put away some liquor! He quite admired him for it. Then Stillman belched and wiped his hand on his sleeve.

"You see you do, hammerhead! Here's a few dollars to keep you keen," he slurred, and tossed a roll over the bar.

Damn, thought Sam, that clinches it. The bugger must be out of his mind to throw his money around in front of four strangers. But Stillman didn't seem to notice the group of men. What the hell was the matter with the bastard?

Sam picked up the roll and stowed

it inside his vest. It would fund his sudden trip from this stinking town.

"Want anything else, Mister Stillman?"

"Nope! I'm going to get me organized, and I'm gonna teach those bloody miners a lesson," he slurred.

Sam realized something he'd never thought possible: Black Jack Stillman was a frightened man.

"How you do that, Mister Stillman?"

Stillman swayed and put a finger to his nose.

"Now that would be telling." He laughed. "You do what you have to do and then stand back and watch the fireworks!"

Sam reached for a glass to polish and nodded, inwardly thinking, you'll be lucky, buster. I'll be long gone from here!

Stillman reached for the bottle again and left the bar with it nearly empty. He could feel the comforting bulge of the other bottle in his pocket and if the fiery urge came upon him he could assuage it at any time. His guts were on fire but his rage at Jeanie and the unknown enemy was subsiding in the merciful haze which was surrounding him.

He knew that he needed this haze more and more. It blotted out all the nightmares of the past few years. He must find the marshal and get that lazy bastard moving. He walked up the street oblivious of those whom he passed. He didn't see those who whispered and wasn't aware of the tension in the air.

Jack Stillman was in the throes of one of his monumental benders. The townsfolk waited. Usually at these times the benders ended with atrocities, like men gunned down openly in the saloons or, worse still, in lonely camps and then would come the steady stream of gold ore brought in to the assayer's office while Stillman's gunnies guarded both the office and the bank next door.

It didn't end there of course. The whole town knew that Stillman was hand in glove with the senator who happened to be a governor of their railway spur and who'd got the line built in the first place and was taking a percentage of the gold taken out. It was an open secret. It was a disgrace. But what could they do about it, until now, that is?

Those who watched Stillman's progress, wondered. What would he do when he knew that Paddy Fyngal was back in town.

Paddy Fyngal was the man who'd got away and made Jack Stillman and his cronies a laughing stock.

Everyone had heard the tale of the minted gold and Stillman's frantic search for the location of that lost payroll.

Black Jack Stillman was an unforgiving man and he had a long memory. Those who knew Black Jack pitied Paddy Fyngal. Someday, somehow, Paddy would be brought in and God help the poor bastard.

The Indian scout called Big Nose watched the big man walk erratically up the street. He smiled contemptuously and allowed the man to pass and then followed discreetly behind. As a scout, Big Nose always knew he had the advantage when he knew something; other men would pay for the information he tucked away behind his black inscrutable eyes.

He knew about Stillman and the barkeeper Sam. He had even fed Sam with false information and got paid for it. He also knew that Sam and Stillman were somehow mixed up with one of the officers back in the fort. He'd watched Stillman arrive and be ushered into the presence of Major Conrad after dark. He'd listened at the major's window without much success, but the furtive way in which the big man had departed showed that something was afoot and it was something not legal. Big Nose was a patient man. He could wait. Someday something big would happen and now, today, he thought this might just be the time.

He was slipping down an alleyway to come up behind the marshal's office when he felt a tap on his shoulder. He spun around with teeth bared and then relaxed. It was one of Hunting Bear's dog soldiers. His eyes flickered.

"You risk much coming here, Mongoose, so it must be important for you to see me. What is it?"

Mongoose looked fearfully around.

"I come and I go, quickly. Hunting Bear wants you in his tepee as soon as possible."

Big Nose cursed and watched the broad back of Stillman turn into the office. He was missing the opportunity to maybe hear what Stillman was up to.

"Will it not wait? I have work to do. I am here on the business of the sergeant in Fort Laramie," he lied.

Mongoose shrugged.

"When Hunting Bear sends out a call, men fly like birds to the roost."

"Do you know why he wants me?"

Mongoose shook his head. "I only

know that he has had big pow-wow with the man called Fyngal and the white men who live in Hunting Bear's village."

"Ah, now I'm beginning to see." He nodded reflectively. No need to explain to the young warrior who was looking distinctly uncomfortable and wanted to be off.

"You may return and tell Hunting Bear I shall be with him as soon as possible . . . before the next dawn breaks."

Mongoose didn't need any more persuading and left at a trot, slipping down the alleyway leading to the back of the marshal's office.

Big Nose paused. He was half inclined to follow up his first idea and then reflected that he might do more good visiting a half-breed he sometimes exchanged information with, and who mined a claim just south of town. It was also in the direction he must go to reach Hunting Bear's village. If anyone knew what was up, then Billy Blackfoot would have some answers.

Billy Blackfoot straightened his back with difficulty. Standing in water and sieving a tin bowl of river mud for a few grains of gold dust each day for more hours than he would ever put in as a cowpoke had put a permanent crick in his back. He wiped his forehead and stared at his friend, Big Nose.

"Yeh, the rumour's true. There's going to be some changes round here, all right, and we're goin' to get a fair deal."

"What's happening?"

"I don't know the right of it but the word's gone out not to take any gold into town."

"And then what?"

Billy Blackfoot looked suspiciously at Big Nose.

"Why you so goddamn interested? Are you for us or against us?"

"I want to be on the side of the winners in this. I've got a meeting with

Hunting Bear and I want answers to questions he might ask."

"Well, if he's involved, tell him we're waiting to act and we're getting impatient."

"It will take time to organize."

"The miners know that. They just want something to give 'em hope."

"Well, they've got that. They say that Fyngal, the man who bested Stillman about the whereabouts of that minted gold he took into town, is being roped in."

"If that's so, you can tell Hunting Bear and his pals we're ready when they are."

Big Nose nodded.

"That's all I want to know. Now I'll be off."

The man who'd followed Big Nose out of town, squatted on his heels and spat on the ground. Now just what had Big Nose and the half-breed in common? One was a military scout and the other a down-on-his-luck miner who could only scrabble a few ounces

of gold dust every week, just enough
to buy him a few supplies. It might
be a good idea to go down and choke
some answers out of the bastard. The
big boss would be pleased . . .

5

THE word had gone out like a forest fire, a ripple of excitement amongst the miners bonding friends and enemies alike in their common hatred of Black Jack Stillman and his hangers-on.

Big Nose had slipped silently into Hunting Bear's tepee and sat cross-legged in front of the old man, his face grave and thoughtful.

"You sent for me, Chief?"

The dignified grey-haired chief smiled and nodded.

"I knew you would come on the wings of the wind when you knew I needed you. I trust your judgement, Big Nose. It is about the black heart, the one who brings death and destruction to the sacred places. You have heard of the man called Fyngal?"

Big Nose nodded.

"Everyone has heard of this man, even the chief's in the fort. He is not a man to have as an enemy."

"Good. For he is to help us to clear our name with the white men."

"And why should he do that?"

"Because we shall help him in his own quest."

"And what is that?"

The chief shrugged. "He does not trust us enough to speak of it, but I know by his eyes he is haunted. He has the look of a man driven beyond rest. Yes, even behind the smiles and smooth talk, he is visited during sleep time with that which troubles him. I know!"

Big Nose nodded. "Then what must I do?"

"You must talk to him and carry out his orders."

"It shall be done."

"And Big Nose . . . " The old man hesitated and then went on, "I understand Mongoose did a good job in finding you. He and his father,

Broken Lance, divided the search for you. The boy was brave to come into town. I want you to take him with you and turn him into a scout. You will do this for my grandson?"

Big Nose was taken aback.

"But Chief I work alone. The danger . . . you understand. I should never forgive myself if I was the means of a Sioux chief's grandson meeting his death!"

"You would not be responsible. It would be the will of the Great Spirit if he was taken from us. There are many ways a youth can prove his manhood and for us now, at this time, it would be a means of helping us in our aims, but also a proving of a future chief. I have talked this over with Broken Lance and he approves. Will you take him with you?"

"It seems I don't have a choice."

Hunting Bear smiled and the craggy face split into many wrinkles like that of aged timber drying out into splinters.

"It seems you do not."

And so it came about that with Mongoose's help Big Nose visited all the main sites of the mines and many of the smaller remote ones, and aimed an arrow that twanged deep into the timber uprights carrying a crude message for all those who could, to meet at the Dutchman's mine in the heart of the Black Hills.

Fyngal and Jonty Randel had laboriously written the messages on the pages of a torn up Bible and given strict instructions for their delivery.

"Now remember, Big Nose, none of those boys must see you or they'll think it a Sioux trick for a bit of massacring. We don't want that, do we?"

Big Nose shook his head, still digesting Fyngal's plan for the shipment of the gold. He wondered what the black-hearted Stillman would think of it if he knew!

"Mongoose and I are ready to go. And after we've delivered all the messages we shall visit the lodges and pass the word that when the moon is three-quarters gone, they shall be ready and waiting to escort the miners' wagons to their hideout."

"Shouldn't they know where they're heading?"

Fyngal laughed and put a finger to his nose.

"Now that would be telling! Just think of it, boyo. All the wagons heading for the Dutchman's mine, all coming from all points of the compass! As long as your Indian friends are hiding out, watching for trouble from Stillman and his crew, they don't need to know information that could cause their deaths if they were unfortunate enough to be caught and tortured by Stillman's gang. You understand?"

Big Nose nodded.

"Understand. No loose talk. No big ears to listen."

"Good. So you can be on your way."

Big Nose was weary. He had jog-trotted for hours, slammed his arrows home and gone on without rest or food. But now he was hoping for a respite with his friend, Billy Blackfoot. He anticipated a long cool drink of Billy's speciality, the pulque made with cactus. He was indifferent to the food he would be given. It was the pulque that mattered.

As he approached the site, his keen eyes looked out for Billy. Nothing stirred and there was no sign or smell of woodsmoke. Big Nose paused and watched, a frisson of awareness rippling up and down his spine. It wasn't like Billy to be far from his claim.

Then he noticed the abandoned rifle. He frowned. There had been trouble here. He stepped forward carefully, placing one foot in front of the other so that he made no sound. He looked into the roughly timbered tunnel where Billy spent his days. Nothing. Then he searched the lean-to where Billy slept and kept his few tools and his pulque and his dried foodstuffs. Again nothing.

He moved to the sluice made of

untreated planks of timber and it was there in the trough below he found Billy . . . a Billy whom he hardly recognized, who'd been tortured and strangled and by the staring eyes, it had been a hard way to go.

Big Nose stared down at the man. It was a pity about him. He had been useful over the years. Now his quick mind assessed what Billy could have told whoever had jumped him.

It was obvious one of Stillman's gang had been out to get information, and as Billy hadn't been able to give him what he wanted, Billy had paid the price.

Quickly Big Nose pulled the already smelling body out of the water and taking time out buried it beneath a scattering of boulders. He had no feelings for Billy, only it was a nuisance that now he didn't have a reliable contact who went regularly into town and listened to the gossip in the saloons. He had been useful on occasion. Big Nose wept no tears for him. The man was in the past . . .

After the chore of planting Billy, Big Nose looked about him for the pulque. It was gone. So the bastard had taken that and the bit of grub Billy had and, Big Nose just realized, he'd taken the donkey as well. Big Nose knew that donkey. It had a scar across his right cheek where a mountain cat had clawed him. He would be easy to recognize again.

So Big Nose did not linger and went on to his next call. He wondered how Mongoose was faring. The boy would sure get some practice in creeping up on a feller.

Mongoose was a cocky young rooster. As he progressed from one claim to another, his confidence grew to foolish proportions. He had no idea of the plans afoot and he knew very little about Black Jack Stillman or perhaps he might have been a little bit more careful.

He squatted behind some scrub and carefully took aim at a crazy-hanging plank door that was swinging from leather hinges from a makeshift lean-to shed. He could see the miner at some distance working for paydirt in the muddy stream some sixty yards away. He was safe. He could plant his message and be on his way to the next stop in a matter of minutes.

The man following him frowned. This young buck might come up with the answers the half-breed wouldn't or couldn't give him.

He was within six feet of Mongoose when the boy whirled at the rustling sound. Ned Symes fired automatically and took the boy in the shoulder. He cursed as the miner ahead heard the shot and, what was worse, several other prospectors working close by came charging down the clearing and Ned Symes took to his heels and disappeared into the scrub.

They found Mongoose, groaning, crouched on the ground like an animal at bay.

"Steady now, boy." The miner whose door Mongoose's arrow had pierced, knelt down beside him to examine the wound. His fingers probed roughly.

"You've a bullet in your shoulder, lad," he said cheerfully, "but you'll live. What the hell were you doing around here? You're one of Hunting Bear's dog soldiers aren't you?"

Mongoose hung his head, more in shame than pain. He could endure the pain but to realize he could let an enemy move up on him so easily filled him with humiliation.

"I come with a message . . ." Suddenly the world went black as the blood poured from him.

Tot Greenwood looked down at him.

"I guess he's one of those greenhorns out to make a man of himself." He spat inches from Mongoose's outstretched hand. "We'll have to drag him into shelter, Jake, and dig out that bullet or he'll die of lead poisoning."

They started to haul him away when a youth ran up waving an arrow and a piece of paper.

"Hey, Tot, there's some kind of a

message here. Can you read it?"

Tot took the crumpled page ripped from a Bible and stared at the writing. He scratched his head and the other men who'd come running at the sound of the shot gathered around.

"Anybody here who can cypher?"

An old grey-haired man with a gaunt face and a gap-toothed grin held out his hand.

"I used to be a teacher back East. I'll read it." He read aloud Fyngal's message. Tot punched the air.

"So it's true! The Irishman's no myth. Let's get ourselves to the Dutchman's mine!"

There was a general shout of agreement and then the old schoolmaster waved his hands above his head.

"Hold it, fellers. Not so fast. We don't all need to go. We've got to guard what we've got. How do we know that Stillman's gang won't pull a fast one when we're gone? I vote we send a couple of representatives and we guard our claims. Remember, none of us have unloaded what gold we have since the word went out."

Tot considered.

"You got a point, old man. At best they could destroy our camps and at worst blow some of the bigger ones up. Yeh, we'll form a kind of committee and the best two men voted in will go. Come on, let's get on with it!"

★ ★ ★

Black Jack Stillman stared at Ned Symes, his little pig eyes spitting fire.

"You fool! You'll have the whole Sioux nation on our backs if they find out who shot that boy!"

"He didn't recognize me, boss. I swear it. He turned so fast I let go before I had time to think. I was lucky to get away at all. The place was crawling with miners. But the fact remains, the boy was delivering some kind of message . . . "

"Then why the hell didn't you wait long enough to search his pouch and

129

see if he had other messages for other miners?"

Ned Symes blinked in surprise.

"Never thought of it, boss. I thought it just a message for one miner, like."

"That's your trouble. You don't think a thing through. You expect me to do all your thinking! My God! I'm blessed with idiots around me! Now I'll have to call in the army for protection and you know what that means . . . sharing with that rogue major and him having a finger on me for the rest of my natural! Damn you Ned, for a moron! At least you could have killed the little bastard!"

"What's a moron, boss?"

"Never you mind, but you are one and don't forget it!"

"Can I go now, boss? Is there anything else?"

"No, just get out of my sight but don't get drunk. I want what wits you've got to be clear during the next few days. Savvy?"

Ned Symes nodded and left Stillman's

office intent on going to the nearest saloon and to hell with Stillman's orders. He could hold his drink and he wanted to ask the barman what a moron was . . .

Stillman tapped the top of the desk with impatient fingers. How to get to know what was going on? He had upwards of thirty gunmen who would put their lives in their hands if he lifted a finger but not one of them had the brains of a louse when it came to intrigue, not even his brother-in-law the marshal, and as for Bill Tomlin, the assayer, he was only interested in gold.

Suddenly he grinned and slapped his leg.

"By God, why didn't I think of her before? If she can't find out then nobody can." He reached for his hat. It was time to go and visit Jeanie and spell out the facts of life and what she had to do . . .

Jeanie looked at him with horror and loathing.

131

"You expect me to damn well take my life in my hands and go horsing around in a rickety coach with only a man dressed as a woman to protect me just so that I can get in touch with either the bloody Indians or that wild Irishman everyone talks about?"

"Irishman? What Irishman?"

Jeanie looked at him with amazement.

"You haven't heard of the Irishman? The man called Fyngal?"

Black Jack swore.

"By God, I'll have someone's guts for this! Of course I didn't know, but I should have done! So it's Fyngal, the bastard who knows where the military payroll is hidden! Now I'm beginning to understand. The marshal must know about Fyngal and maybe he's holding out to find the cursed mick for himself. Who else knows about him?"

"Why, everyone I guess. Why worry about him, anyway? He's just a feller with a gift of the gab."

"Don't you see? He's the one who's banded the miners together. I want

132

him, Jeanie, and you're the one to catch him for me. Savvy? Even an Irishman must have his weak points."

"Then what would you do with him, *if* you caught him?"

"There'll be no ifs. If you can't snare him I'll find other means and when I get him . . . " he paused and Jeanie saw the wild predator gleaming from his eyes "I'll drag the whereabouts of that gold out of him by fire if necessary."

"Then afterwards?"

"I'll string him up. What else?"

Jeanie felt sick. Her flesh crawled. She'd made her mind up. She would go on that coach and get out of town and stop out.

She smiled.

"Then I'll go along with your plan. You'll have to tell me exactly what you want me to do."

"Good. Now this is how I planned it . . . "

133

6

THE wagons rolled at night over little known trails and all converging on the Dutchman's mine, the old played-out claim in the Black Hills. As each miner arrived he found his own hiding place for horses and wagon. Then, shouldering his bags of hard-earned gold he joined the growing band of men waiting for the night of the three-quarter moon.

They were a quiet subdued bunch, joining their own acquaintances and gathering in groups. There was no liquor drinking and each man was tense and looking for assurance amongst his fellows.

There were doubts raised and a few heated arguments about the merits of bypassing the gold assayer and his Gold Corporation and sending their gold out of the territory in this newly formed co-operative movement all explained by Jonty Randel and his boys.

The idea had been new and startling but the more they talked about it, the better the idea seemed. But there were still diehards who found it convenient to go into town, sell their dust and go on the razzle, get blind drunk and if they were lucky get a quick fumble with one of the saloon girls, and if there was any cash over, take back some meagre supplies that would last until they'd scraped up another few ounces of dust, all the while hoping and praying for a big nugget, or better still finding signs of a motherlode . . .

All those who could be there, were there on the night of the three-quarter moon. They waited quietly in the light of many small fires and from a distance, the fires looked like fireflies flickering in the night sky.

Fyngal, drawing up his horse, watched from a distant peak. He wondered just where Hunting Bear's braves would be holed up. Along each trail he hoped, but he was having to take the chief on trust. But if he judged the man correctly, he was too proud to let a white man down. His men would be there, waiting.

His eyes skimmed the valley floor below. There was movement down there. He could see what looked like a long distance travelling coach moving along the silvery strip of road leading away from Harper's Creek. He had a gut feeling about it. He knew no miner would own a coach and four horses, besides, they'd had orders to keep away from the main trails.

A thought struck him. Could it be Black Jack Stillman himself up to no good? His imagination took over. A coach that size could hide a light machine gun and a couple of soldiers to use it. He expected Stillman to bring in his cronies from the fort. That was what he would do if he was Stillman.

He didn't doubt for an instant that Stillman knew who he was up against.

He'd have it figured by now and the thought of catching Fyngal would be like a red rag to a bull.

Fyngal smiled. The cache and Fyngal himself would bring out the major and his men like flowers in spring.

He watched as the coach drew nearer and then spurred his horse into action and picked his way down the steep incline, sliding and leaping until he was on the trail some way ahead.

The horse's bellows heaved as he waited for the lumbering coach to come up over the last ridge and gallop down towards him. He heard the rasping of brakes and the driver's cursing as he hauled on the reins to stop. The four horses snorted and steamed, probably thankful for the rest.

"What the hell you want?" bawled the driver.

"Who've you got aboard and why travel at night?"

"Mind your own business. I've only two women aboard and I'm not carrying gold if that's what you're holding us up for."

Fyngal inched his horse forward until he was opposite the door of the coach. "I'm not after gold. All I want is to see who's in there."

The curtain across the door window was twitched aside.

"As the driver said, sir, he is only carrying two women," and Fyngal saw Jeanie Gleeson's bright blonde hair and it looked like silver moonbeams to his bemused gaze.

"I'm sorry, ma'am, if I've frightened you . . ."

"Not at all, sir. I'm not frightened. Should I be?" She opened the door and stepped down, a vision in blue velvet with a saucy bonnet swinging from ribbons down her back. It looked as if she'd dispensed with it for comfort so that she could doze.

Behind her came a tall gangling creature dressed entirely in black and still wearing hat and veil. She looked slightly ridiculous. Fyngal barely glanced at her but put her down to being the lady's chaperone.

The young lady smiled and waved to the coach.

"Please, look inside. There's nobody else."

Fyngal coughed. "I don't doubt your word, ma'am. I'm sorry I stopped you."

"You needn't apologize. I can take the chance to stretch my legs as can my maid. Do you want to take a walk, Betsy?"

Betsy didn't speak but bowed her head and walked away and disappeared behind a boulder. No doubt she was taking the chance to relieve herself, Fyngal thought practically.

"May I know who you are?" Fyngal heard the lady ask softly.

"Paddy Fyngal at your service," he grinned.

Jeanie liked his grin and all the rest of him. He was a big improvement on Black Jack . . .

"I'm Jeanie Gleeson and heading as far away from these damned Black

Hills as I can get. Gold! You can keep it!"

"I gather you haven't done too well in Harper's Creek?"

Jeanie coughed. She wondered just how much this man knew about the affairs of Harper's Creek. She took a chance.

"I'm a schoolma'am, would you believe? And I thought Harper's Creek would be a real town with a church and a school and such and I was wrong. There's no families and the only females are saloon girls, so I couldn't stay, could I?"

She smiled winsomely at Fyngal.

"No ma'am. Whoever persuaded you to come into the Black Hills did you wrong. Well, I wish you luck and hope you find what you're looking for . . . "

"Raise your hands, big feller, or I'll drill you in a place which won't kill you but will cause a lot of pain."

The voice came from behind Fyngal and as he could see the driver still holding his reins and waiting to proceed, he knew it must be the woman in black, but the voice was that of a man!

He raised his hands and froze and became aware of searching hands, that took away his gun and felt around for any other weapons. His eyes caught and held Jeanie's.

"Why? Is this a new kind of hold-up? Are you reckoning on robbing the robber?"

"No!" She turned away, unable to meet the accusation in his eyes. "It's not like that."

"Then what is it?"

"Black Jack wants you. I've made a deal with Mitch here. He'll take you back to Harper's Creek and I'll go on to Laramie."

Mitch had shed his woman's clothes behind the boulder and was now revealed as his true self. He quickly tied Fyngal's wrists to the pommel of his saddle and his feet under the horse's belly.

141

Fyngal cursed his carelessness but the woman's hair had distracted him away from the one he'd dismissed as just an old woman. He was more humiliated in his pride than worried about a confrontation with Black Jack. He knew that Mitch was in for an unpleasant surprise.

"I'm sorry Fyngal," Jeanie's voice came clear in the night air. "I wish you luck!" and she climbed back into the coach and slammed the door. "Ready, Danny? We'll be on our way!"

Danny let off the brake and gave a great yell.

"YAH!" He hauled on the reins and the horses strained and the cumbersome coach started to roll.

Mitch leapt up behind Fyngal and dug his gun in his back.

"Come on, feller, let's go see the boss." They headed back along the track towards Harper's Creek.

The track wound around and about to bypass huge boulders and old workings and Fyngal's quick mind decided where the place would be if he was to get some help. He was watchful as they approached the gully which had once been a natural split in the rocks, then washed away by water countless thousands of years ago. It was a place about twelve feet wide with rearing cliffs at each side. The ground was smooth and sandy, a relic of an old river bed, washed clean by the long gone water.

This was the place he would jump a man if he had the choice. He waited, every nerve and sinew tensed and ready. The ropes binding him to the pommel were gradually loosening with the movement of the horse. He had been working his hands at every lift of the saddle. Only his feet were clamped fast and unable to move.

He knew what he should do if he got free. One sharp dig into Mitch's groin and he could just about grasp the knife that the man carried in a pouch at his waist.

Then, exultation swamped him. Two

things happened: strands of the plaited rope gave and he could turn his wrists, and Sol's voice from behind them froze horse and men in their tracks.

"Get down off that horse, mister, nice and easy. I've got my sights right in the middle of your back where it'll do most grief."

Fyngal felt the shock go through the man behind him. With a wrench that nearly took his hand off, he freed himself from the loosened ropes and reached for the knife before Mitch could recover from his surprise.

He lashed out backwards and caught the man's thigh with a sharp uppercut movement that sliced the flesh from the bone. Mitch groaned and flopped to the ground.

Sol walked up to the fallen man and turned him with the toe of his boot.

"He'll live if the coyotes don't find him." Then he grinned at Fyngal. "I never thought to see you hogtied. How come?"

"Aw, it's a divil of a tale, it be, it be and not worth the tellin'. Just unloose my bloody feet before they drop off me."

A couple of swipes with his knife and Sol had him free and Paddy was groaning and working his feet to get the blood moving again.

Then when he was feeling better and had drunk half the liquor in Sol's hipflask, he said suddenly, "You all alone? I thought you were the one who liked company."

Sol shrugged eloquently and silently pointed upwards and Fyngal saw the figure of an Indian sitting crosslegged on the top of the highest peak just above them.

"I might have guessed it! You won't stir an inch in these hills without someone holding your hand!"

"No need for insults, you bog trotter! If it hadn't been for Broken Lance, I would never have known what happened to you."

"Then why didn't you do something

sooner, or don't your wits work at night?"

Sol laughed, not in the least put out by Fyngal's bluster.

"Broken Lance was intrigued by the woman going behind a boulder and peeling off her clothes."

"You was watching all that?"

"Yeh, and you making a fool of yourself over the blonde female. You must have done to be taken in," he said, as Paddy reared up in a fury to protest. "How the hell anyone could mistake that scumbag to be a woman beats me. You could tell by his walk."

"Oh, shut your face!"

"And then there was all the fancy talk . . . "

"I said shut it!" Then Fyngal smiled. "She was gorgeous. I wonder who she really was? Here, give me your hand, pard. I'm sure grateful, that I am, I am, but no more about it, eh, or I'll smash your face in!"

They grasped hands and then Sol gave a whistle and Broken Lance came down the rocks like a muskrat and joined them.

Broken Lance's sombre face broke into a grimace that Fyngal took to be a grin. He was irritated afresh.

"Now don't *you* start, redskin! Even an Irishman can make a mistake!"

"But not know man from woman . . . " Broken Lance's sharp intake of breath while he shook his head, said it all.

"Oh, go on wid yer! You're both a pair of ugly spalpeens! No-one would mistake the pair of you for wimmen!" The brogue was more pronounced. Sol took note. He could gauge Paddy's temper by his accent. Now it was time to pour oil on troubled waters.

"Aw, forget it! You weren't to figure on a man in a woman's skirt. It's like not figuring on a bullet whamming you in the back! Come on, let's get to that meeting and sort out what those fellers are willing to do."

Down at the Dutchman's mine there were more than a hundred men and they were only the representatives of their pards and neighbours. All were eager to strike a blow against the bloodsuckers who were siphoning off more gold than the men who dug the stuff out from underground or painstakingly sieved and riddled gold dust from the shallow streams.

A great shout went up on their arrival and Fyngal raised both hands above his head for quiet. The glow from the leaping flames from many small fires lit up expectant faces. A great hush descended on the crowd.

Then Fyngal along with Jonty Randel explained the plan and that the men could decide whether to go along with it or be responsible for their own gold. The men listened and formed small groups to talk and argue the merits of banding together, allowing Fyngal and Randel to take charge and hide their gold and to fix a time when the entire wagon train of raw gold would be transported to what was commonly known as the 'gold spur' to connect to the newly opened Union Pacific

Railroad. But there was a lot of terrain to cover before the gold could be safely stowed aboard the custom-built bullion coach. It was this factor that the men argued over. To trust the long haul, or bow to the inevitable and sell their gold in nearby Harper's Creek to the corrupt Gold Corporation. At least they were guaranteed some money in return even though Black Jack Stillman and his cronies got a goodly percentage.

The argument was still raging next day, but there were some already in favour and Fyngal and Jonty Randel were already taking tally of each man's haul, which might be a few pitiful ounces to a load that might break a mule's back.

As the men watched the queue to join Fyngal's plan grow longer, it influenced the doubters more than words and most capitulated and waited their turn.

It was one of the doubters who gave the alarm. Tom Jenks had loaded up ready to return to his claim, reckoning he couldn't wait the length of time it would take before he saw his cash. He needed money right now for supplies, so he was going back to the same old routine of submitting his gold to the assayer and taking what he offered and then paying off the storeman what he owed and then getting new supplies on tick. It was the only way he knew and it suited him.

But when he breasted the first rise and saw the kick-up of dust in the early morning light, he knew Fyngal hadn't lied the night before when he'd told the men to expect trouble from Stillman and his men.

He hauled on his reins and stopped. Screwing up his eyes to see better, he waited until the early morning mist cleared and watched the long straggle of riders coming lickety-split along the valley floor. It was when he recognized Black Jack's sturdy bulk riding the distinctive black stallion that he turned and whipping up his mules, rode as if the Devil was after him.

His headlong gallop and the dust

his rickety wagon tossed up, alerted the men who crowded round when he finally pulled up with a mighty screech of wheels and brake.

Fyngal, with Sol right behind him, was the first to greet him.

"What is it, man? What's happened?"

"You were right," Tom Jenks panted, great globules of sweat running down his cheeks. "Black Jack's on his way. He's not going to let the miners have their pow-wow. He's coming furious and fast and he's got an army of men riding behind him!"

Fyngal frowned.

"You mean the military, so soon?"

Tom shook his head. "No. His gunnies. But they're just as good as or even better than those rookies out of Fort Laramie."

Fyngal turned to Sol and laughed and it was a wild sound and full of confidence. Sol's heart leapt. Fyngal was the man to follow.

"What did I tell you, Sol? There was only one way to lure Black Jack out into the open. Gold, my boyo. Gold is the big man's downfall. You'll see," and he slapped Sol on the shoulder which made the smaller man stagger back and wish his pard wasn't so exuberant.

Fyngal's stentorian yell soon had all the men listening avidly. Those who had weapons and knew how to use them were to gather under the leadership of Jonty Randel and his boys. The old and defenceless were to get into the old mine where their gold was now being stashed ready to be taken by night to Fyngal's own hiding place.

The men with Randel dispersed and hid behind outcrops of rock ready to take action when necessary. Fyngal himself climbed high on to a promontory and soon located the long string of riders. As they neared he counted at least sixty horsemen and knew he'd lured the whole nest of vipers out into the open.

Then, as he expected, he heard the

drumbeat. It was a deep menacing tone that caught at the heart in its sheer unexpectedness. It was echoed from each surrounding peak as if the drums talked to each other.

One of Randel's miners was crouched not far from him.

"That's Sioux war talk. What in hell's started 'em off now?"

Fyngal grinned.

"They're our secret weapon, mister."

"You were expecting them?"

"Aye, that I was! We Irish might be wild but we're not fools! We don't go into battle if some one else will do it for us, an' all an' all!"

"You're a fly one, Mister Fyngal."

"Just call me Paddy, boyo. With a bit of luck there won't be many of that lot get through to butcher fellers more used to shovels than rifles!"

As they watched the riders draw closer, the drumbeats grew louder and more frenzied until the vibrations hurt the ears, and then suddenly the surrounding hills on either side of the valley vibrated to the echo of answering drumbeats. They were light almost musical notes and the deep bass drum ceased as suddenly as it had begun. Then came the silence as if the earth and all on it were listening.

It was eerie.

It was menacing.

Fyngal hauled himself up from his hiding place and looked for and found the rising dust of the oncoming men.

"They're coming in much slower now," he said over his shoulder to his companion. "The drum message has got to them." Then, as he watched, the pace quickened and they were coming on again at a thundering rate. "The spalpeens sure are confident of themselves, bedad! Each and every one of the blackhearted mob must be a professional killer to underestimate Hunting Bear's drum, the divil take 'em!"

"What will happen now, Paddy?"

"The sons of bitches are in for a nasty surprise. Those besoms aren't goin' to be after murderin' fellers who only use picks and shovels as weapons, they'll be up against Hunting Bear's picked warriors. They've been mighty quiet for the last few years and will be itchin' to have a go at Black Jack's mob. Hunting Bear is a proud man and he'll not forgive bein' blamed for somethin' he didn't do. It'll be a Sunday afternoon picnic for his boyos!"

Sol and Jonty Randel crawled up beside the two watching men.

"What's happening?" Sol asked, breathing heavily.

Fyngal explained and Sol let out a breath of relief. He wasn't cut out for fighting professional gunnies and his guts settled down to their usual level.

"Thank God for Hunting Bear," he breathed softly.

Fyngal grinned.

"No fear of crapping yourself now, Sol?"

Sol flushed. "I'm not a fighting man, Paddy, but I would have done my best."

"It's not over yet, boyo, so don't get too cocky. There's many a slip, as my dear old mammy used to say."

"Why? What could happen . . . " Suddenly Sol stopped speaking as he watched with some fascination what was happening down in the valley.

Suddenly from every piece of cover, a man arose and the oncoming untidy string of horsemen were surrounded by warriors. High on a peak the deep bass note of the drum vibrated and then the war cries came, bringing ice to the heart of all who listened.

Jonty Randel pointed.

"Look! Up there," and they saw on the highest peak the huge drum swinging on wooden supports and the feathered drummer who swung the huge club with measured strokes.

"He's directing the battle," Fyngal said shrewdly. "Look down below at their tactics. Each brave knows exactly what he's expected to do!"

They watched the sudden sharp infighting. The gunnies' rifles were hardly used, and the men were so rattled their hand guns fired and missed as they were pulled from milling horses and rolled to the ground in a frenzied attack.

They watched in awe at the fighting rage of Hunting Bear's braves.

"Bejasus, I'm glad they're on our side!" Fyngal muttered aloud.

Behind them a cheer went up. Fyngal turned and saw a crowd of miners perched on ledges and watching the action. He waved and they waved back. He smiled.

"A good bunch of boyos and I bet they could do some damage with their shovels if they were up against it, by damn!"

"Some of them are getting away!" Jonty Randel yelled, and Fyngal turned sharply to witness a sudden exodus of riders streaming back along the way they'd come with some of the fleetest Sioux runners racing behind, only to stop at intervals to fire a well-aimed arrow.

Then the small bunch were disappearing around a cluster of rocks. Fyngal swore luridly and long.

"It looks as if Black Jack might have got away."

Sol, silent and thoughtful up until now, said, "He got away. I recognized his horse. What do we do now?"

"Get the gold train away. He'll be back and he thinks the miners' gold and the military payroll are stashed in the Dutchman's mine. He'll head back here, so we've got to get moving!"

He paused to watch the action down below. It was all but over. It had been short and sharp. He could see a number of bodies lying and riderless horses being chased by Indian braves. He saw odd puffs of smoke as despairing gunnies emptied their pistols before being struck down. It was a massacre and Fyngal felt no pity for the professional killers.

Then down below it was all confusion. Three overland wagons were loaded up with sacks of gold ore and dust.

Each man received his receipt from a sweating Sol and a grinning Randel, while Fyngal gave instructions for them to get back as soon as possible to their claims and defend them from Black Jack who was even now most probably thinking of revenge.

So the miners rode away in their now empty wagons. They were conscious of keen eyes watching as they followed the trails. Fyngal, with Sol and Jonty Randel and his boys were also conscious of unseen guards. The clumsy wagons made slow progress but apart from one broken axle which had to be fixed and a foundering horse as they crossed the fast-flowing Hidden Rocks river, they came at last to the waterfall ten miles upstream. There they stopped.

Jonty Randel looked at Fyngal in surprise.

"This is the place?" Fyngal nodded. "You would never believe it, would you?"

Jonty Randel spat on the ground and looked about him. He saw the

159

rising cliffs running into a deep gorge. The ground was rough and steep with scrub. Great chasms split the earth and dominating the scene was the waterfall that gushed out from amidst the jumble of rocks that appeared to have been dropped from a great height.

"I can't see no caves or such," he began and Sol nudged him. Fyngal had already entrusted him with the secret, and Jonty stared at the waterfall itself.

"You mean it's in there?" he gasped.

Fyngal grinned.

"Would you like to go and find out for yourself?"

"Hell no! I don't fancy swimming those rapids. I'm no white-water man. I haven't the legs for it! How come you found this place?"

"We're not far off the trail that leads to Laramie. One of the soldiers with me knew the region. He got killed, poor bastard, but he did me a service. It was hard but we managed it."

"And we've got to do the same thing?"

160

"You won't. Sol and I will. You sit tight until we return."

"You don't trust us?"

"There's four of you and only two of us. I don't fancy bein' bushwhacked even though we've got company. Those braves might think it part of the plan if you turn on us. After all, you're their pals not ours!"

"Well, I'll go to hell!"

"You probably will, eventually."

"It never crossed our minds, did it, fellers?" The others looked stolidly at Randel and shook their heads like puppets.

Fyngal gave a slow grin and looked meaningfully at Sol. So this was what Paddy had meant by it not being over ... Sol coughed to give Paddy the signal that he understood, which Paddy had had the forethought to think about days before.

Sol counted to three and then his hand flickered and his Colt was in his hand. He might be no good at the physical stuff but he could handle

161

his gun like an old friend. At the same time Fyngal's gun appeared and Randel and his men were looking helplessly down both barrels.

"Now I don't want to argue the point, Randel, and I don't say you're a liar, but just to make sure, we're gonna tie you up while you have a nice rest. No hard feelin's, pard, just bein' cautious like."

"Why, you bastard!"

Fyngal laughed.

"You forget, I know you, boyo from the past. You didn't expect I would offer you a gold bonanza on a plate? I'm no bogtrotter with less wit than the village idiot! You'll get your share and so will these bums of yours." He nodded to Sol. "Fasten 'em up tight, boyo and then we'll be on our way."

"I'll get you for this, Fyngal!"

"Why? I aim to make life easy for you. We do the grafting and you enjoy the proceeds."

"Wait until I tell Hunting Bear how you've treated us!"

"He'll approve, my big-gob friend. He'd consider I was a fool if I didn't take precautions."

He watched while Sol did an efficient job of immobilizing them while listening to Randel's lurid cursing and then smiled as Sol gagged Randel with his own dirty neckerchief.

"There, that will keep the bastard quiet," Sol remarked with a gleam in his eyes.

"Come on, we've wasted enough time on this lot."

Sol followed Fyngal to where the wagons stood. They then quickly unyoked the mules and proceeded to transfer the miners' gold in their sacks to the backs of the animals.

Then, tying each mule to the tail of the next, they led them down the steep path to the river below and walked the little cavalcade up the middle of the river bed towards the waterfall. The mules were hard-pressed to hold their footing as the water ran swiftly and wet their underbellies.

"Why can't we just travel along the riverbank?" gasped Sol as he was dunked for the second time.

"You'll see," Fyngal shouted grimly, "this is the way we brought the military payroll, and we're right on target!"

And so they were, for as he spoke the current swept both horses and men towards and under the waterfall as if in a great whirlpool. Coughing and choking, both men scrambled on to a wet ledge and as each mule shot into the comparative calm, hauled and pulled the frightened creatures on to the broad slate ledge where each mule stood quivering and snorting.

At last all mules were bunched together, giving off steam and slipping on the smooth water-worn stones. Fyngal moved forward with the leader and Sol waited and came behind as he watched each mule move ahead.

Then Sol got the surprise of his life. In the greeny-blue dimness dappled with sunshine, Sol saw the huge cave-opening that was completely hidden by the curtain of water. He shivered, for it was cold and dank and moss and growing vines were a natural camouflage. He would never have known the opening was there if Fyngal hadn't gone straight to it and torn down the creepers which were growing over the opening.

Inside the cave it was dry and large enough to take all the mules and as many more again. Fyngal groped and found a lantern he'd placed there when the payroll was stashed. In the flickering light, Sol looked about him and saw the cave paintings etched in red and black.

"This place is one of the sacred sites," he breathed in awe. Fyngal nodded complacently.

"It certainly is and what's more, it's supposed to be cursed and no Indian will come within miles of it. Couldn't be better, could it? Black Jack would never find it in a month of Sundays!"

"But what about getting it out? Aren't there going to be problems?"

Fyngal put a finger to the side of his nose.

"I explored this place when I planted the payroll. It was to escape the Indians. I found an old riverbed and followed it and would you believe, it came out not far from the rail spur. We're home and dry, boyo."

"But what about Randel and his boys?"

Fyngal gave Sol an amused glance.

"What about 'em?"

"Well, you did say they would get their whack. You gave your promise," Fyngal grunted.

"I'm not out to cheat the miners or Randel. He might be as mad as a hornet but his cash draft will be waiting for him along with the miners when we make delivery."

"But what about Black Jack?"

"Think about it, Sol. He'll be making post-haste for Fort Laramie, if he hasn't already sent off a messenger. They'll follow our tracks, for Hunting Bear's people won't be able to stop them.

Besides, Hunting Bear doesn't want to tangle with the military for political reasons."

"So you think they'll find this cave?"

"Nope!"

"But they will. They'll not be stopped by taboos."

"They won't be for they won't even get behind the waterfall, and for why? Because all along that river bank will be miners who've got the whole ground in front of them sown with dynamite. There's no one can handle dynamite like a miner can. I left instructions that when we got the gold away, they would follow and lay their dynamite and when the gallant Major Dwight B. for bastard Conrad comes galloping to the rescue, hopefully he'll lose more than just a limb, for the whole world will go up!"

Sol laughed and looked at Fyngal in admiration.

"You think of everything, pard. I'm glad I'm with you, not against you, that I am."

Fyngal shrugged.

"Let's get on our way."

The tunnel led into an ages-old, dry riverbed and they traversed it for nearly a mile before it suddenly opened out into blinding sunlight. Then it was easy going picking their way through outcrops of rock and scrub and finally hitting the road that ran alongside the railway spur.

They waited nearly a full day before they heard the whistle of the oncoming train. Fyngal stood out on the track waving his arms. He heard the squeal of brakes long before the train was upon them. He helped Sol quieten the frightened mules and waited.

It was quickly done, the transfer of the gold into the official security guard's care and as Sol was going along to see safe delivery Fyngal gathered up the receipts for the gold and the ore and was reasonably confident that all would be delivered safely. He sighed with relief, for the rest of the payroll had gone too, hidden in the miner's sacks, and he knew the man who was to take delivery would do it, without too many questions being asked.

He rode one of the mules on the return journey, the rest following behind for the miners would want their mules returned.

Now Fyngal could put his whole mind on Major Conrad, the man who had killed his brother.

7

MAJOR Dwight B. Conrad drew rein as soon as he recognized the big man, Black Jack Stillman. Why the hell was he and some of his raggle-taggle gunslingers coming hell for leather towards him? They should have been giving those damn miners a lesson they wouldn't forget. His lips curled disdainfully. He would soon put some starch into the men just as he had done with his own troops. He raised an arm and the column stopped behind him, glad of the rest for they had travelled at a punishing rate and as the sergeant muttered to his corporal, the horses' legs would be shot before the battle commenced.

Black Jack's horse reeled drunkenly and he cursed. His own mount had been arrowed under him. The arrow had narrowly missed his thigh, but he didn't appreciate his luck, he just cursed that he had had to make do with a lighter, inferior pony that he'd caught when Two-draw Pete was flung into the air with an arrow sticking through his right eye.

The major stiffened his back and raised his chin. He was a fierce looking man in his early forties, and his moustache and chin whiskers, greying a little, did nothing for his appearance. He scowled at Black Jack, and expected the same reaction from him as he did from his own men, but Black Jack scowled back and went on the offensive.

"Where the hell have you been? You're not riding to a Sunday hoedown. I expected you at the Dutchman's mine before dawn!"

Major Conrad shook with anger, he couldn't believe what he was hearing. If it wasn't for the fact that Black Jack and he had created a somewhat shady alliance so that he had a nice nest egg for an early retirement, he would have been ranting him off a strip and then leading his troops back to the fort and to hell with the foul-mouthed bastard.

"I might have crack troops, Stillman, but we can't fly," he said with tight-lipped irony. "Your messenger only arrived, half dead I might add, two nights ago, having had to dodge some of Hunting Bear's people. As it was, he took an arrow in a shoulder. Well? What's happened? It looks like you've been routed by a bunch of miners."

"Not miners, damn them, but Hunting Bear's braves. We had no idea . . . "

"No? That shows lack of leadership, Stillman. You should have waited for us professionals to do the job. You should have at least sent out your scouts to assess the situation."

"I have no scouts," Stillman grunted. "We just did as usual, went in for the kill. After all, they were only unarmed miners."

"And were they?" Major Conrad asked keenly.

"As far as we know they haven't anything more lethal than a pickaxe. We never got near enough to find out. Those goddamned Indians seem to rise out of the ground."

"Now I wonder why they should be rising at this time? Hunting Bear's been living quietly for quite a time. I thought skirmishes with the Sioux were things of the past."

"Well, I assure you they're on the rampage. Why? I don't know, unless that Irish blackguard has something to do with it."

"Or you've blamed the Indians once too often for your killings and you've brought this on yourself!"

There was mockery in the major's tone that didn't go down too well.

"You're blaming me, eh? Well, all I can say is that you're in danger of losing a half share of that gold same as me and must I point out that there's still that payroll to locate? That bloody Irishman could lead us to it."

"What Irishman?"

"Why, the bloody feller who's stirring up these miners. You don't think they have a leader amongst them with enough brains to figure out a way to bypass the Gold Corporation, do you?"

"Hm." There was a distinct intake of breath and Stillman watched curiously as Major Conrad stared into space and saw something only he could see. He had gone white under the whiskers.

"You all right, Major?"

"Hm? What? Oh yeh, yeh. Just thinking. Tactics, you know."

But Black Jack knew he was lying.

"It wouldn't be tactics against Fyngal would it?"

The major stared at him.

"Fyngal, you say? I once knew a doctor of that name."

"Well, it can't be Paddy Fyngal. This Fyngal is an ex-soldier and the first I knew of him he came toting minted gold into Harper's Creek which was mighty fishy but before I could do anything about it, he'd scarpered. My men went after him and got themselves shot up. Somehow, he got to the miners and the bloody Indians and now we've got a full-scale war on our hands."

"You shouldn't leave all the graft to your men. You should have killed him yourself."

"How did I know he would turn out so dangerous? Bloody hell! I'm not a fortune-teller!"

"All right! All right! Let's forget it and think of this new situation. We'll want another troop of men so I'll send a messenger back to the fort and then we'll go and surprise these bloody miners and find us some gold!"

The major signalled to his sergeant and gave his orders and then he raised an arm and the rest of the little expedition moved forward. Stillman watched him go. Arrogant bastard, he thought. One of these days he would break that stiff back of his, and he, Stillman, hoped he would be there to see it.

Stillman and his men were in no shape to follow. The horses were tuckered out and most of the men had minor wounds from the Indian charge. They had little food and no water, so they hunkered out in the scrub and hobbled their horses near some scant vegetation. The major could carry the offensive alone. He had the men and the weapons and as he said pointedly, he had the expertise. Let him get on with it!

* * *

Dawn was breaking when Paddy Fyngal and Sol Klein along with Jonty Randel and the Jordache brothers, released earlier with much swearing on their part, hit the camp. Jonty Randel was the first one to send a bullet into a blanketed figure to send him to Hell. He hoped it would be Stillman but it wasn't. It was the red-headed devil who'd built the fire and helped to torture Willy Jordache before they cut out his tongue.

Then the whole camp exploded into gunfire as blanketed men struggled to find weapons and roll into the scrub while Randel and his boys stood around firing as if at rats caught in the remains of a haystack.

Sol reluctantly lifted his weapon to fire. He had no heart for this kind of execution. He would stand his ground with any man in a fair fight. This was just murder.

Fyngal's arm came up and stopped him. He looked at Paddy in surprise. Fyngal shook his head.

"This isn't our fight. This is what those boyos have lived for. We can only watch."

Sol nodded and sheathed his weapon.

It was soon over, but not before Charlie Jordache caught a slug in the throat from a lucky shot from Stillman. Willy too was hit and bleeding badly, but he struggled to a sitting position and took what looked like a drunken aim with a gun that was fast growing too heavy to handle. With a supreme effort, he took Stillman in the middle of his broad back. He watched the big man collapse like a deflated balloon before slumping forward with a fixed grin on his face. The gun dropped by his side.

Fyngal looked at Sol.

"Well, that's it then, execution's over. We'd better go and see what shape Randel and Jordache are in."

Randel was exhausted but not hurt and Ned Jordache had a graze on his temple. He would never be so near death again. Randel grinned up at Fyngal.

"We did it, and it was fitting that Willy did for Stillman in the back. Couldn't have been better." He coughed and breathed hard. "It don't do much for me, however. I've still got this wrecked body. Will you see to Ned?"

Fyngal nodded and bound Ned's head with his own bandanna to stop the bleeding and the attracting of flies.

Sol got on with digging a grave big enough to take two. The other bodies could rot where they were and make a meal for the coyotes.

When all was over, they prepared to depart and Fyngal's head came up and he was sniffing the air to the south.

"Now we go after Major Conrad."

Randel was quiet on the return to the Sioux village. It had been decided between them that Randel was in no shape to continue the offensive. He and Ned would go back to their old life . . . indeed that was what they wanted.

He looked up with an effort at Fyngal riding quietly beside him.

"You know something, pard?"

"I know lots of things, boyo."

"Well, I just want you to know I trust you, even though you did the dirty on us about the gold, and I can't say I've said that to many people in my life, especially white men. Even Ned, I don't go a hundred per cent."

"What's this spiel leadin' up to, boyo?"

"About the gold . . . "

"Ah now we have it! Come on now, spit it out!"

"I know you'll do right by us. That there gold . . . "

"Yeh, you and Ned will get your whack or my name isn't Fyngal."

"That's all I wanted to know."

"And you'll get Charlie's and Willy's and Parker's too, God rest him! I thought maybe it might fall lucky like into Hunting Bear's hands. It could do some good there." His eyes twinkled. "After all, it's come out of his land!"

Randel stretched out his hand.

"Put it there, pard, I couldn't have said it better myself. There's a squaw who looks kindly on me . . . "

"Then make her happy, boyo. I wish you luck!"

There was a surprising number of miners waiting at the Dutchman's mine when they returned and with them was Broken Lance with his son, Mongoose, and a number of braves.

Broken Lance stepped forward to greet Fyngal and Sol. He stood tall and dignified and it passed through Fyngal's mind that he would make a good chief when his father decided to head for the great hunting ground in the sky.

It was good to have such a friend.

"We have talked with the miners and now they know that it was not of our doing that men died violently. We know that these men have lived within the law that is made in Washington and that none of our sacred places have been violated, so, we are prepared to fight alongside these men and to stop Major Conrad's troop from getting back to Fort Laramie."

"You would fight the military? That would be taken as an uprising of the Sioux. It could have terrible results."

Broken Lance shrugged.

"What will be, will be. Someday it must come, but maybe not yet. The major travels fast but he is only a few hours ahead. I and my braves can travel secret trails and be waiting for him in the Great Buffalo Pass which he must travel to return to the fort. We shall hold him up and you and those men who can fight will follow behind and you can do with the major as you wish. We shall remain in the background."

"No! I have a better plan. Sol and I shall come with you and we leave the miners to go back and do what they do best. I'm not interested in the troops. All I want is the major!"

He grinned wolfishly, his lips curling back from his teeth showing white amidst the coarse black beard.

Sol, watching intently but silently, felt a frisson of horror run up and down his spine. This wasn't his pard, Fyngal whom he looked to and admired. This was a grieving brother eaten up with the poison of revenge. What horror had he conjured up for Major Dwight B. for bastard Conrad?

"Paddy . . . " but Fyngal waved a

182

hand dismissing the protest on Sol's lips.

"You're with me, Sol? You and me are pards. You wouldn't let me down?"

Sol shook his head, mute. Who was he to judge another man's ache for revenge? It wasn't his brother Major Conrad had killed.

"Good. Then all we have to do is talk to the miners and tell them what's happening and that soon as possible they'll all get their bankdrafts and their mutiny is over and Stillman dead."

There was a great cheer when the news was broken to them and most of those who stayed behind now hitched up their wagons already eager to get back to work.

Two miners built like wrestlers however looked like staying a little longer. They came over to Fyngal's campfire while he and Sol were eating and oiling their weapons.

"What you have in mind, mister?" the older man of the two asked. "You didn't give us the whole story did you, mate?"

"I did as far as you're concerned, boyo. What I do now is my business."

"The others seem to go along with what you said. How do we know we can trust you? You could be heading out with all our gold dust and leave us all cleaned out of what we've worked for all these months." He turned to his mate, "Isn't that right Pete?"

"Yeh, that's right. We figured you was no goddamn do-gooder. Who in hell would get off his arse to help someone else?"

"You've just met someone, boyo. As you know, I'm an Irish bogtrotter and Irish bogtrotters are all mad and unpredictable and we all stick together. That's the way we survive. Now as I figured it, there being no other bogtrotters around, I find me another bogtrotting family. Right?"

"Well, what do you mean by that?"

"That I object to what you're implying, buster! I look after my

184

own!" and with that, Fyngal took Pete in the belly so that he jack-knifed forward and caught him a hammer blow with an iron fist. Pete gagged and groaned and as Sol pulled his gun, Fyngal launched himself at the first man who was slowly getting his wits back at the sudden onslaught.

Sol watched as the stranger took a pummelling. No need to worry. Fyngal was a dirty fighter and he had everything in hand. Sol's main worry was if Pete decided to join the fun. But Pete was still gasping to get his wind back and was disinclined to be a hero.

Sol started to worry when Fyngal took two hamfisted blows to the kidneys that made him grunt. The giant miner might be slow-witted but he'd had experience in bar-room brawls and he was coming on fast. He took a blow to the chin and stood like a sturdy tree and shook his head and came on at a rush with a piledriver that would have taken off Fyngal's head if it had connected.

But Fyngal saw it coming and ducked and came up with two blows to the ribs that would have cracked them if the feller hadn't had such a beer gut.

Now they were both down and rolling in the dirt. Blood spouted and Sol wasn't sure who was bleeding the most. He considered firing a shot and stopping the carnage but he knew Fyngal wouldn't be best pleased. This was his business. He'd started it and he would finish it.

The end came suddenly. The miner clawed the ground and came up with a rock as big as a man's head. He crashed it down to where Fyngal's head should have been and wasn't for the Irishman had lunged and rolled to the right and in that infinitesimal second while his opponent struggled to raise it again, Fyngal drew up his legs and kicked out with all his might. One boot caught the man fair in the forehead and he rolled away like an overstuffed rag doll. The fight was over.

Fyngal sat up, head streaming with

blood, his chest heaving and globules of sweat coursing down his forehead and stinging his eyes. He wiped away the sweat with a bloody fist.

"That was a rare fight! It reminded me of Saturday nights back in County Cork. I could do with a drink, I could, an' all, an' all." His brogue was accentuated, his eyes gleamed and Sol marvelled. The crazy fool was actually enjoying it all!

Silently Sol offered the bottle he'd kept hidden for emergencies. He wasn't quite sure whether this was an emergency or a celebration. However, the bloody bottle was fast emptying.

"Should we do something about these guys?"

"Why?" Fyngal grunted. "Let sleeping dogs lie. They'll only suffer when they come to." Sol shrugged eloquently. He was good at that.

"Then you might as well hand that bottle back. I could do with a drink myself."

Fyngal took another swig and then

grudgingly handed it back.

For all the punishment Fyngal had taken, he was ready and waiting when Broken Lance came to announce that the time was right to move out. The moon was high and the hidden trail easily traversed and they would travel swiftly while the major and his troop bivouacked along the trail. Broken Lance looked at him and nodded.

Fyngal nodded in return. There was no need of speech. He and Sol followed the Indian swiftly to the corral where the Indian ponies were kept, ready for instant action.

"You both take Indian pony. More used to hill travel than your horses," Broken Lance waved to the milling animals. "Choose whichever you wish." Fyngal, who had a small sack with him, slung it over his shoulder and dived for a black and white pinto that looked big enough to take his weight.

He would have to ride without a saddle for none of these wild mustangs were broken as a white man would break in his horse. He welcomed the challenge, but for Sol it was a different matter. He liked his horses with irons and a decent saddle. He reckoned his was going to be one hell of a trip and he wished it over. However, he managed to catch and hang on to his chosen steed and throw a leg over and then settle back and cling on to the mane of the animal until he could master the rawhide lead rope looped about mouth and head.

They moved swiftly and crossing the mountains and gulleys and keeping to the higher ground was not such an ordeal as Sol had envisaged. Once they trod water and moved slowly upstream until they came to a rocky ford and surfaced with ponies shaking off rivulets of water and moving sure-footed over wet slabs of granite while overhead rose sheer cliffs that could never have been traversed.

It was with surprise then that Broken Lance pulled up and pointed out the row of tents in the far distance. They were high up on a peak and the first rays of the sun hinted at a new day. It was a pinky gold and at any other time, Sol would have enjoyed the vista of the sun turning the rocks and vegetation into a rich molten glow.

But his attention was on the camp and on the one soldier who seemed to be on guard duty, and he appeared careless as if the duty was only a token arrangement. Fyngal smiled at Sol, voicing what Sol was thinking.

"Very confident they seem. I think the major needs a lesson in controlling discipline. A sloppy commander means sloppy men! However, I'm not complaining."

Broken Lance turned sharply to him.

"The plan goes ahead? You want no killing?"

"That's right, Broken Lance. No killing. Just get that major out for me without causing a fuss and I'll be in your debt for life."

Broken Lance nodded.

"It can be done. Mongoose can take the man on guard. He is like a snake in the grass and I and two of my men will bring you the major without any of the troops being disturbed."

"You're sure about this, Broken Lance?"

The Indian gave Fyngal a pitying glance.

"I could creep up on you, even though you knew I was coming, at any time I wished. The Great Spirit makes me invisible!"

"Hmm, well I don't know about that, but if you say so, it must be true."

"Do you want me to demonstrate?"

"No, bejasus! Just get on and do the job!"

Broken Lance gave them a rare smile and then disappeared into the scrub followed by two of his companions. The other Indians settled themselves to wait. They knew that at a prearranged signal, they would be down here amongst the white soldiers if things went wrong and they would die in defence of their leader.

Fyngal and Sol hobbled the ponies and climbed to a ridge where they could watch the camp without being seen themselves in the event of prying eyes.

They waited anxiously but nothing occurred and the sun came up stronger and higher in the sky. Then as Sol watched, something strange was happening. He could no longer see the lounging guard and yet nothing stirred. Sol let out a deep breath. He hadn't realized he was holding his breath.

"Look, something's beginning to happen!"

Fyngal complained there was nothing to see.

Then a soldier came out of one of the tents and stretched and then wandered off into the bushes. He came back and with braces dangling and shirt open he sluiced himself in a small stream close by. Another man appeared and this time kicked the still warm embers of a wood fire into a blaze and fed it with scrub and dried grass before wandering into the scrub to relieve himself.

"Bejasus! The whole damn camp's going to be up and doing before Broken Lance does the job! I thought the bastard was being too confident! We'll have to go on down there, the whole bang lot of us and take him by force! That we will, and the divil take it!"

"Hey! Wait a minute! Something's happening." Sol caught Fyngal by the shoulder as he was in the act of swinging away to go to the waiting Indians.

They stared down below and saw a soldier come out of the biggest tent of all. He was waving his hands and shouting and all those inside the other tents scrambled out to see what the commotion was about.

Fyngal stared and then shouted and waved his fist into the air.

"Holy Joseph and Mary! The spalpeens have done it! They must have or that there soldier boy wouldn't be makin' such a song and dance! I didn't think Broken Lance would do it! By God, I didn't! If ever he comes back into this world, I hope he comes as an Irishman."

Mongoose slithered into the waiting group and with a few words to the Indians who started to grin, he came and stood by the two men. He grinned at them.

"I put the guard to sleep. He'll have a bad headache but he'll be fine. My father, he comes soon."

It was two hours before the Indians brought in the bedraggled figure of the major. He wasn't much of a man without his uniform. He was wearing woollen combinations and no boots and his face was streaked with blood and one eye was closed. He'd evidently put up a fight once away from his camp.

When he saw Fyngal, his eyes snapped their fury.

"This is an outrage! Kidnapping an

officer and taking sides with Indians is treason and you'll suffer, I swear it, if it takes the rest of my life!"

"It might do just that, Major." The major blenched.

"What do you mean by that? Do you mean to murder me after those animals have amused themselves torturing me?"

"Those days are long gone, Major. The Sioux in these parts live a law-abiding life if left alone. Of course they don't like taking the blame for murders they didn't do as Stillman found to his cost."

"But that has nothing to do with me! Whatever he chose to do was none of my affair!"

"No? But you knew of it and turned a blind eye! You also took bribes. Don't try to deny it, Major. We've got a list of your deposits at the bank in Harper's Creek." Fyngal smiled at the major's expression. "Oh yes, we've got our contacts just as you have, Major."

"What are you going to do with me?" He swallowed painfully. "Doctor?"

"Ah, so you do remember. I was thinking that after a lifetime of dirty deeds, you might not remember the butchering you indulged in thereby causing my brother's death!"

"You let *my* brother die!"

"That was unfortunate but I did everything to keep him alive. You on the other hand . . . " Fyngal stopped and turned away, suddenly overcome with the old anger and grief.

Sol watched him. He knew Fyngal was at breaking point. He gestured to Broken Lance.

"Take him away and tie him up out of his sight, or else he's going to bring himself down to this pig's level!"

Broken Lance nodded and dragged the major away into the scrub where he was securely tied and Mongoose ordered to watch him for any tricks.

Broken Lance returned to Sol.

"What do we do now?"

"We wait."

"Wait? The Sioux do not wait when the enemy is for the taking."

Sol grimaced.

"Are you forgetting something? You are not at war. This is the Irishman's business. We wait until the panic is over down there and the sergeant orders the return to the fort. Savvy?"

Broken Lance shrugged.

"You are all crazy men, but I wait."

"Yes, you do that, pal. We need your escort for what that crazy man means to do!"

Broken Lance raised his eyebrows in a question but Sol turned away and stared down below at the bunched up soldiers. He wished he knew what the sergeant would decide to do. It didn't take long. After searching the perimeter of the camp in careless fashion, the sergeant's stentorian voice came faintly on the breeze. The tents came down, the fire was doused and they saddled up and were soon on their way as if the Devil was after them.

Fyngal laughed and slapped Sol's shoulder.

"See, I told you so. That sergeant

didn't think much of the major or he would have ordered a more thorough search. He did just enough so that the men could verify that there was a search. Now all we have to do is follow behind, an' all, an' all!"

"Are you sure about this?"

"As sure as I'm sure I'm goin' to Hell!"

Sol nodded. That figured.

"Right. I'll go and round up our friends. They're itching to get a move on."

"Yeh, it's time to put Broken Lance into the picture."

"I think he was for changing his mind and going home. This up and coming chief likes action. When Hunting Bear dies, there could easily be another uprising."

"Hm," grunted Fyngal, "that's not our problem. What we want is a band of Indians with the guts to escort us into the fort and get us out again without bloodshed. Get Broken Lance and we'll talk."

Broken Lance's eyes gleamed at the challenge. This was one way to show the white men that the Sioux couldn't be intimidated by any show of force and they could ride proudly into the very fort itself. Besides, it gave those young braves with him a chance to test their merit.

"Then we make war?"

"Not unless the soldiers are foolish enough to strike the first blow."

Broken Lance looked disappointed. He shook his head.

"You crazy man."

Sol agreed with Broken Lance but Fyngal just laughed.

"First, we shall send in a messenger on the heels of the troop before a search party can be sent out."

Sol looked at him curiously. This was something new.

"Why the messenger?"

"Because I want the major's wife and daughter to come out and meet us and I want you, Sol, to be the messenger!"

8

THE little party watched the coach wind its way along the dusty trail, sometimes being lost behind rearing boulders and at other times bouncing over the rough terrain.

Fyngal and Broken Lance watched in silence until they could see Sol Klein sitting on the box seat and wielding the whip.

Sol looked calm and relaxed as he handled the reins. Fyngal stepped out on to the pinnacle of rock and waved his arms. Sol answered with a flourish of his whip. That was the private signal between them that all was well.

He and the Indians scrambled down the incline to where their ponies were tethered and they were astride and waiting when the coach drew near and stopped.

Fyngal dismounted and gave his reins to Broken Lance and shouting his approval to a grinning Sol, opened the coach door and surveyed the two frightened females inside.

"Hello, Mary. It's been a long time!"

Mary Conrad leaned forward.

"So it *is* you! I couldn't believe it. What do you want with us, Doctor? What do you want with me and my daughter?"

She was a comely woman, a little plumper than when he had seen her last and her daughter, Sarah, was now a grown woman. Mary's dark hair was tinged with grey and the laughter lines he remembered were now . . . what? He wondered how the major had treated her. He balled his fists. If she hadn't already been married when they'd first met, he would have married her himself. It would be God help the bastard if he'd made her unhappy.

He glanced at Sarah with interest. She would be going on sixteen by his reckoning. A sweet-looking creature, very like her mother. He felt shame at bringing these two into his revenge plan. But he'd made a vow and it must be kept.

"You will know I have the major prisoner?"

"Yes," answered Mary in a low voice. "Your man explained that if Sarah and I did not come then he should die. So I am here. What can I do?"

"I want you to persuade your husband to leave the army. I also want you to persuade him to confess to the killing of my brother and the reason he had me struck off the register of medical practitioners and how he lied and covered up what happened. I want him to do it in front of the whole garrison of Fort Laramie. I want everyone to know what a cur he is. Will you do this?"

"And if I don't succeed?"

"Then I'm afraid, ma'am, you will go back to Fort Laramie as a widow and your daughter will be an orphan."

She turned very white and Sarah thrust her head into her mother's shoulder.

"I'm frightened, Mama, please do as he says."

Mary put her daughter from her and prepared to step down from the coach. She ignored Fyngal's hand to do this and Fyngal knew that any friendship between them was gone forever. He hardened his heart. The bastard major was going to have to pay!

Broken Lance flung the wrist-bound major at Fyngal's feet and Fyngal hauled him upright and he stood facing his wife, his daughter cowering in the coach.

The Indians, smelling of buffalo fat, crowded round to witness this white man's justice. They didn't know what to expect.

They waited.

Mary looked at Fyngal. "Does he know?"

"No. You must ask him."

Mary then explained what must be

done and Major Conrad stiffened in fury.

"The man lies! Goddammit, Mary! Whose side are you on?"

"You told me that Liam Fyngal died of wounds and you never told me why Doctor Fyngal left so suddenly. You said he deserted. What really happened, Dwight?"

The major stared sullenly at her.

"It's none of your business, Mary! He's a lying murderer . . . "

"Careful, Major. You're not in a position to shout your mouth off," Fyngal's voice cut in, cold and menacing.

"I'll bloody well shout all I want! There'll be a detail out looking for me and believe me, they'll not leave one of you alive! Not one stinking son of a bitch alive, you Irish cretin, you traitor, you Indian lover who crawls at their level!"

Broken Lance stepped forward and his fist connected on the major's jaw lifting him high into the air before he fell with a dull thud to the ground.

Fyngal turned him over with his boot. He was out cold.

"You didn't do a good job, ma'am. I think other tactics are called for. I'm sorry."

"What are you going to do?"

"What I should have done at first, ma'am." Then he nodded to Sol who climbed down from the coach.

"Bring the girl out and tie her up."

"What?" gasped Sol. "What are you going to do?" Fyngal's eyes did not meet his.

"You'll see." He took hold of Mary. "I'm sorry it's come to this," and he proceeded to tie her wrists together.

Then the major was roughly brought round. He groaned and shook his head as he was hauled upright. He stared hard at Mary and Sarah who were both fastened to one of the wheels of the coach. Sarah was crying aloud. Mary was white-faced but silent.

"What are you going to do with them?" he whispered hoarsely.

"Just one of them, Major. Just one of

them and you are going to choose which one. You will have that privilege." Fyngal's voice was silky soft.

"For God's sake, spell it out!"

"Very well. As you don't relish the idea of confessing your crime and circumstances to your peers in the fort, I thought maybe we should dispense some of your own kind of justice."

"I don't know what you mean!" But his face blenched as he spoke and he turned to look at Fyngal with horror. Fyngal nodded.

"Yes, go on, Major, tell your wife and daughter of the notion that has just popped into your mind."

"You devil! You couldn't possibly . . . they're *women*, for pity's sake! If you must butcher someone, then let it be me!"

Mary looked at first one and then the other.

"I don't understand."

Fyngal couldn't bear to look at her. He spoke roughly. "He does, ma'am. Now choose, damn you!"

The major recoiled and suddenly his face screwed up and he wept.

"For God's sake! I beg of you!" and he was kneeling on the ground in front of Fyngal. "Have pity! I could never choose . . . "

"Then I must do it for you," and Fyngal nodded towards Sarah and Broken Lance thrust her forward, after slicing the ropes tying her to the wheel.

"Untie her wrists," said Fyngal, and brought forth the major's own sword. "Is this the same sword, Major, you used on my brother?" It swished through the air as he tested it for speed and balance.

The major groaned while Mary realizing with horror what was happening, screamed and struggled to free herself from the wagon wheel.

"Don't hurt my baby! Take me, but don't hurt my Sarah!"

A nod to Broken Lance and Sarah was on the ground, her arms out-stretched and pegged down with a forked stick. Then Broken Lance was holding her struggling body.

Fyngal was wielding the sword, when the major lunged upwards, grasping the knife out of its sheath from the crouching Broken Lance. It sped handle over blade, bright in the sun, until it embedded itself in Fyngal's chest.

He was dead before he hit the ground and before Sol got the major in his sights and blasted the life out of him. It was over and Sol felt sick. Never in his life would he ever make up his mind whether it had been one crazy bluff or whether Fyngal would have truly done what he threatened.

Sometimes in the years to come, he would cogitate and wonder as he managed the bank in Harper's Creek. He was a popular man and the miners were all prosperous in that region, for Fyngal's gold had put them all on easy street.

For himself, he knew his life had changed from the moment Fyngal had come scrambling up that cliff with his saddle-bags full of minted gold.

But he had never foreseen just how much or that in time he would become a respected citizen and mayor of Harper's Creek. Or that he would step into Black Jack Stillman's shoes and even take his woman. For Jeanie Gleeson had come back to town in all her glory when she heard of the death of Black Jack.

It was a good arrangement. He would never marry her. He would be hogtied by no woman. But he was fond of Jeanie and she was sensible. She knew men didn't marry her kind. They enjoyed each other's company and Sol's guns had soon made it plain that he might be a little man but he could protect his own. So Jeanie felt secure. She grew fat and lazy, contented with things as they were, and as Sol liked a woman with a bit of flesh on her bones, they settled down to make a good life for themselves in Harper's Creek.

It was only at night when Sol couldn't sleep that he sat in his rocking chair on the porch of the fine new house he had built on the outskirts of the town that he thought of Paddy Fyngal, the crazy Irishman and the only friend he'd ever had and sometimes he wished for the old times, when they'd hunkered down in makeshift camps and he'd experienced the true meaning of friendship.

He would always be grateful to Paddy Fyngal.

It was then that he would take a short walk in the moonlight and go on up Boot Hill and come to stand opposite the rude cross which bore the inscription, *Paddy Fyngal, saviour of this town*.

He would talk to him and then with a clear mind walk back to his fine new house ready for another day.

FIGHTING RAMROD
Charles N. Heckelmann

Most men would have cut their losses, but Frazer counted the bullets in his guns and said he'd soak the range in blood before he'd give up another inch of what was his.

LONE GUN
Eric Allen

Smoke Blackbird had been away too long. The Lequires had seized the Blackbird farm, forcing the Indians and settlers off, and no one seemed willing to fight! He had to fight alone.

THE THIRD RIDER
Barry Cord

Mel Rawlins wasn't going to let anything stand in his way. His father was murdered, his two brothers gone. Now Mel rode for vengeance.

ARIZONA DRIFTERS
W. C. Tuttle

When drifting Dutton and Lonnie Steelman decide to become partners they find that they have a common enemy in the formidable Thurston brothers.

TOMBSTONE
Matt Braun

Wells Fargo paid Luke Starbuck to outgun the silver-thieving stagecoach gang at Tombstone. Before long Luke can see the only thing bearing fruit in this eldorado will be the gallows tree.

HIGH BORDER RIDERS
Lee Floren

Buckshot McKee and Tortilla Joe cut the trail of a border tough who was running Mexican beef into Texas. They stopped the smuggler in his tracks.

BRETT RANDALL, GAMBLER
E. B. Mann

Larry Day had the choice of running away from the law or of assuming a dead man's place. No matter what he decided he was bound to end up dead.

THE GUNSHARP
William R. Cox

The Eggerleys weren't very smart. They trained their sights on Will Carney and Arizona's biggest blood bath began.

THE DEPUTY OF SAN RIANO
Lawrence A. Keating and
Al. P. Nelson

When a man fell dead from his horse, Ed Grant was spotted riding away from the scene. The deputy sheriff rode out after him and came up against everything from gunfire to dynamite.

FARGO: MASSACRE RIVER
John Benteen

The ambushers up ahead had now blocked the road. Fargo's convoy was a jumble, a perfect target for the insurgents' weapons!

SUNDANCE: DEATH IN THE LAVA
John Benteen

The Modoc's captured the wagon train and its cargo of gold. But now the halfbreed they called Sundance was going after it . . .

HARSH RECKONING
Phil Ketchum

Five years of keeping himself alive in a brutal prison had made Brand tough and careless about who he gunned down . . .

FARGO: PANAMA GOLD
John Benteen

With foreign money behind him, Buckner was going to destroy the Panama Canal before it could be completed. Fargo's job was to stop Buckner.

FARGO: THE SHARPSHOOTERS
John Benteen

The Canfield clan, thirty strong were raising hell in Texas. Fargo was tough enough to hold his own against the whole clan.

PISTOL LAW
Paul Evan Lehman

Lance Jones came back to Mustang for just one thing — revenge! Revenge on the people who had him thrown in jail.

HELL RIDERS
Steve Mensing

Wade Walker's kid brother, Duane, was locked up in the Silver City jail facing a rope at dawn. Wade was a ruthless outlaw, but he was smart, and he had vowed to have his brother out of jail before morning!

DESERT OF THE DAMNED
Nelson Nye

The law was after him for the murder of a marshal — a murder he didn't commit. Breen was after him for revenge — and Breen wouldn't stop at anything . . . blackmail, a frameup . . . or murder.

DAY OF THE COMANCHEROS
Steven C. Lawrence

Their very name struck terror into men's hearts — the Comancheros, a savage army of cutthroats who swept across Texas, leaving behind a bloodstained trail of robbery and murder.

SUNDANCE: SILENT ENEMY
John Benteen

A lone crazed Cheyenne was on a personal war path. They needed to pit one man against one crazed Indian. That man was Sundance.

LASSITER
Jack Slade

Lassiter wasn't the kind of man to listen to reason. Cross him once and he'll hold a grudge for years to come — if he let you live that long.

LAST STAGE TO GOMORRAH
Barry Cord

Jeff Carter, tough ex-riverboat gambler, now had himself a horse ranch that kept him free from gunfights and card games. Until Sturvesant of Wells Fargo showed up.